The ETCH Anthology 2018

Vocamus Press – Guelph, Ontario

ISBN 13: 978-1-928171-70-6 (pbk)
ISBN 13: 978-1-928171-71-3 (ebk)

Produced by Vocamus Writers Community

Vocamus Press
130 Dublin Street, North
Guelph, Ontario, Canada
N1H 4N4

www.vocamus.net

2018

CONTENTS

GRADES 11 - 12

GRADES 9 - 10

GRADES 7 - 8

Sponsors

ETCH 2018 is produced by Vocamus Writers Community, a non-profit community organisation that supports book culture in the Guelph area.

This season our work was generously supported by June Blair, Nick Dinka, Alec Follett, Andrew Goodwin, Paul Hock, Jaya James, Michael Kleiza, Sheila Koop, Garth Laidlaw, Jane Litchfield, Marian Thorpe, and Mark Whoachickie. We appreciate their support very much.

If you'd also like to support the work of Vocamus Writers Community, you can find us on www.patreon.com.

Acknowledgements

The stories in this collection are the winners and runners up from the Guelph Public Library's 2018 Teen Writing Contest. They were judged and arranged in the collection by grade level.

The cover of the collection was made using the winning entry of the Guelph Public Library's 2018 Cover Contest, created by Sandhya C. Seeram, a Grade 12 student at Guelph Collegiate Vocational Institute.

Writerly mentorship was provided by local authors – Justin Admiral, Phil Andrews, Kayla Besse, Melinda Burns, Anthony Carnovale, James Clarke, Kathryn Edgecombe, Nikki Everts, Gloria Ferris, Martina Freitag, Kristen Forbes, Darcy Hiltz, Paul Hock, Christy Howitt, Laura Lush, Kim Davids Mandar, Kat McNichol, Shane Neilson, Corrie Shoemaker, Robert E. Simmons, Bieke Stengos, Autumn Walker-Duncan, and Donna Warner.

The Teen Writing Contest was organised by Elissa Davidson of the Guelph Public Library. The ETCH Coordinator for Vocamus Writers Community was Maria Stengos Camamert. The stories were judged by Elissa Davidson, Jeremy Luke Hill, and Maria Stengos Camamert. The book's cover and interior were designed by Jeremy Luke Hill of Vocamus Press.

GRADES 11 - 12

1st PLACE

The Greatest Fool of All

Katherine Zhang

She sits alone at the top of the stairs. Strong marble pillars arch elegantly overhead, firmly supporting the high ceiling. Brilliant beams of sunlight sweep through the tall glass windows. And yet, a seeping chill penetrates the grand hall, one that not even the summer sun can kiss away.

The hall holds no unnecessary décor. No tapestries display the ruler's conquests, nor are there places for light to shine come nightfall. Only a thin strip of blood red carpet disrupts the monochrome, snaking from the entrance to the very back of the room. It flows over a long flight of stairs to the throne.

The ruler stares straight ahead as a sly smirk dances over her thin ruby lips. Her legs dangle over the armrests and her silken dress pools in rivulets on the floor. A facade of nonchalance permeates through her posture, but fierce eyes dispel the illusion. She is not one to let down her guard so easily.

"Who's approaching? Go on, name yourself," she calls out to the intruder. Met with a deathly silence, she rights herself and straightens out her spine. This ruler refuses to be toppled by a simple assassin. She's been taught better than that.

A sudden involuntary shudder rips through her body, and she berates herself for losing composure so easily. But old habits are not easily broken, especially those that had been ingrained into her very being since her youth.

Her eyes dart to the ceiling, where a well-concealed automatic rifle awaits. One could not be a supreme ruler without first making a few enemies. And she would much rather be feared as iron-fisted than have her reign cut tragically short.

She'd installed autonomous weapons at throughout her castle. Not to mention all of the hidden trapdoors and trick rooms incorporated into the floor plan. How, then, with all these precautions, could an intruder sneak inside her palace in the first place?

"I suppose I must applaud your persistence in finding your way inside." Though she sees no one, she continues to speak. "Now, I'm not sure if you encountered any of the security features on your stroll, or if you simply took them all down. I'd be quite grateful if you could point out some of my weaknesses."

A soft pinging noise echoes from behind a pillar, and the ruler already has her hand on a gun hidden in the folds of her dress. She contemplates calling the guards, but ultimately decides that this game of cat and mouse is much more amusing.

"Don't pretend you're not there. I can see you." She extends a single finger to the pillar in question. But when there's no response, she retracts her arm, and a delicate frown blooms across her face. She rises and, ever so slowly, descends the staircase. With each step of her heeled feet, she sinks into the plush carpet. All the while, the ruler maintains a steady gaze on her target.

"You do realise you should be afraid of me, right? Even with all of the world's approval, you still won't be able to assassinate me." Her words linger for a moment before vanishing into the emptiness of the room. Still nothing. No response, not a single hint that anything is out of the ordinary. She lets out a hollow laugh despite the precarious situation. Maybe her self-inflicted isolation is making her hallucinate.

No, wait. That thought was wrong. Who in the world had said she was going insane? No one! There were only two people in the throne room.

Right?

Right?

In a sudden fit of desperation, she storms to the pillar and whips out her shotgun with frightening speed, pointing it at the supposed target. "Aren't you afraid of me? Well, if you aren't, you should be. I could end you right now if I wanted to!"

Much to her horror, there is no one behind the pillar. With her heart racing in her throat, she repeats to herself, I'm imagining it. There's no one here, I'm fine, I'm safe, no one's going to hurt me, if I just keep this up for a little longer –

Until she hears it. A metallic sound directly behind her back.

Eyes glinting wildly, she whirls on the spot, where she is greeted with the polished steel of a sword. Her lips pull back into a demonic snarl. "I should have expected you to come."

The mysterious figure moves the blade to the ruler's quivering throat before speaking. "Are you sure I'm the one who should be afraid of you? I could end you right now if I wanted to." Using the exact words the ruler had used mere minutes ago, the assassin steps ever closer, pinning the ruler's back to the marble column. There would be no running, not this time.

The assassin readies the sword for a final swing, but the ruler is faster than anyone could have imagined. A furious and well-placed kick knocks the sword clean away, and the assassin instinctively fall into a diving roll to avoid a maelstrom of bullets, ducking wildly left and right, to find refuge behind one of the marble columns. The sword lies abandoned.

"How dare you! Playing god as if the entire world was your personal chessboard! Do you have any idea how many people are suffering because of you?" The assassin lashes out not with a weapon, but with words instead.

It was the truth. The ruler had introduced many reforms after taking over government in a completely democratic way. She had criminalised all forms of discrimination, and for her efforts she was considered by many to be a kind leader who never went back on her word. Unfortunately, most of the citizens were unaware that their young leader was now resorting to more and more extreme measures for the "greater good of humanity".

"Playing god? As if!" The ruler grits her teeth as she advances on the assassin's hiding place. "I'm just re-enforcing the Golden Rule – do unto others what you want done unto yourself. It's simply justice." Her heeled foot stomps on a hidden panel as she passes by, setting the final piece of her trap in place.

"Who determines that you're doing the right thing? How can anyone trust that you won't turn on the innocent -- so long as you achieve your noble ideals in the end?" With the ruler drawing ever closer to the pillar, the assassin feels assured of victory, unsheathing a knife and leaping in the ruler's direction...

Only to find a gaping hole where the ruler had been, a long fall, and a sudden landing.

The assassin turns looks upwards, unable to comprehend what has happened.

There the ruler stands in all her majestic glory, suspended in midair through the support of a swing. Her white gossamer gown floats behind her, like an avenging angel. The brilliant summer sunshine sets her face aglow, radiant and ethereal, as if she is illuminated by a halo of light.

The ruler mouths, "I win." Or at least that's what the assassin believes she said. But it matters not what words were spoken. The assassin had lost everything. Unable to form the words out loud, the assassin curses the ruler, feels the floor give way, and falls deep below the castle.

"How foolish." The ruler peers into the pitch black abyss with an indulgent grin. "Never assume your victory until your enemy has been destroyed."

And then, as if she had an epiphany, she bitterly laughs. "Oh, but what human isn't a fool?" The young ruler recounts all of the times she had believed in the intrinsic goodness of humanity. Her naïve hope had quickly been snuffed out by the horrific truth: that the lies and selfishness of humans far outweighs their kindness and charity, and that darkness can be found even in the purest of hearts.

"Well, it turns out that I might be the greatest fool of all. What kind of person could possibly hope to destroy all traces of evil in this world without first becoming evil herself?"

2nd PLACE

Andrea

Emily Berry

At the side window of the second floor of the house Justin sets up a folding chair. He sits for five minutes, watching the car next door start on its own. In thirty seconds, Mr. Case will come outside and sit in the driver's seat. It will take another minute or so for Andrea to lazily jog through the garage, open the car door, and tap her boots off so the snow doesn't get inside.

Justin walks casually downstairs to grab his coat, listening for the sound of his school bus pulling away outside. He picks up his shovel once the coast is clear and makes quick work clearing his driveway, the one to the left of his, and Andrea's. Had he just walked across his lawn to her house, he'd make footprints. Had he cleared only her driveway, it would be suspicious. The easiest way to hide was behind a shield of kindness.

Justin strolls across the empty driveway, able to type the garage code in confidently. He's watched hand movements for weeks, every afternoon when Andrea got home. The door begins to open, and he slips underneath it before it's even halfway up, making it close immediately behind him. The door that leads into the house is unlocked, welcoming him. He knows just where to go: left, upstairs, left, straight to the purple bedroom at the end of the hall.

What catches his eye today is her photo wall. She looks beautiful in every one, especially the one with her sisters. Andrea is the prettiest; her cheeks are pinkest, her hair is blondest. She's the best in every way.

He walks over to her bed and presses the balled up sheets to his face. He's overwhelmed with the smell of lavender. It must be from her body wash; she always showers before bed.

In her closet he digs through piles on the floor, plucking out a neglected turtleneck tee shirt. It smells like her. Not the body wash but the natural scent of sweat on skin.

Justin leaves the way he came, turtleneck now tucked into his jacket. He's left lots of time. No one will notice his visit. Back in his own house, he places the shirt in a shoebox, along with the pair of socks and the lip balm that he snatched from Andrea's top drawer last Thursday. He sets his alarm, spends the rest of the afternoon napping, not having much else to do on school days. He has lots of time to waste before 3:36.

At 3:30 Black Veil Brides scream, and Justin's up and walking before his body has even adjusted to being awake. He reclines in his window seat, kicking his feet up onto a stack of pillows that are too flat to sleep on. Pulling out his phone, he taps in his passcode. He types a quick, "hey" to start the conversation.

Out his window, he watches Andrea's lips thank the bus driver on her way out. She walks toward her house. Justin looks up at the clock dangling on his wall – 3:39. He watches it for the next few minutes, having nothing else to look at in his room. In a pile on his floor are all the posters that were torn down eight months ago. Since then his walls, bedsheets, and carpet have all turned grey.

It takes about ten minutes for her to respond to his messages, or at least that's how it's been going for the past week or so. Before that they used Instagram to talk. Justin had spent months working on an account for "Katie Locke", filled with pictures of food, sunsets, and Starbucks. Two weeks ago he commented on one of Andrea's public posts about how excited she was for the new Avengers movie. It was something along the lines of, "How do you feel about Tom Holland as Spider-Man???" After that Andrea sent Katie a message, and they'd been texting ever since.

Andrea: Hey!

Katie: How was your day??

Andrea: Got my calc test back.

Andrea: Rough. You?

Katie: Same. My mom sent me a ham sandwich :O=

Andrea: Ewwwwww

Justin rolls over on and grabs the TV remote, putting *Deadpool* on Netflix. He'd never been able to watch it before. Last year he asked a kid from school to go see it with him, but Justin's dad wouldn't let him go. It took three weeks for him to say more than a word at a time to his dad, and by the time he got back to full sentences it was too late. During the fourth week Justin found him out cold in a bathtub full of blood.

Katie: What's your favourite food?

Andrea: Haha um... mashed potatoes and gravy! Why??

Katie: Idk I just want to get to know you better :)

Andrea: Okay well then how about you??

Katie: Pizza obviously! ;P

He gets up and walks to the kitchen. He can't see Andrea from here, but he can watch her light up the back deck when she flicks on the pot lights in the kitchen. She'll grab a snack from the fridge and then go sit in the living room.

Andrea: Haha okay

Andrea: My turn then. Hmmmm

Their game goes on, Justin collecting information as he goes. He finds out her birthday, where she'd like to travel, her most embarrassing memory.

He opens the door to his backyard, slides on his sandals, and walks out onto the snowy deck.

Climbing onto the railing, he holds the tree trunk for balance. He crawls into the tree and over the fence between their houses, usually spending an hour or two in Andrea's old treehouse. It blocks the wind so it isn't as cold, and he has a perfect view into her living room. He prefers when she's in her bedroom because she's more vulnerable there. In the living room she's used to people being with her. Her bedroom is private. It's 3:52.

Katie: Have you ever kissed a guy?

He watches her through the window, wringing his hand, biting his lip. She doesn't move much.

Andrea: Well duh! I have a boyfriend!

Andrea: You??

Justin slowly puts his phone down on his leg, his whole body shaking, trying to keep himself under control. He forces himself to breathe slowly.

Katie: Woah what?? You didn't tell me you had a boyfriend! Who is he??

Justin pulls his arm out of his sleeve, biting down hard on the fabric of the coat. He can't scream. He'd be caught.

Andrea: Well you probably wouldn't know him. He goes to my school.

Katie: What's his name?? What's he like???

Andrea: Brock! He's super sweet! We've been dating for two weeks!

Justin climbs back over the fence into his backyard and goes inside, snow melting off his shoes onto the floor. Connecting to the wifi, he pulls up Andrea's Instagram page. He clicks on her followers and types the letters B-R-O-C-K so hard he could crack the screen. Only one account comes up. The biography under his name is the school Andrea goes to. This can't be happening.

Katie: Awww that's awesome! I just checked out his Instagram! He's so hot!!

He walks over to the sink, slamming his fists on the marble. He turns on the cold water and lets it run over his hands. She betrayed him.

Andrea: I know! He's coming over for dinner!

Justin wipes his hands on his jeans.

Katie: Ooooh when's that?

Eyes glazed over, he goes into the kitchen and grabs the keys from the counter. He opens the garage and climbs into his dad's car, trailing the slush in with him.

Andrea: Probably soon! I guess I'll have to go then :(

Justin backs out of the driveway and drives all the way around the cul-de-sac before reaching the stop sign at the exit. It's 5:06. Waiting, he pulls out his phone.

Katie: Oh awesome!

A car drives up the road on Justin's right. Its left turn signal comes on just before the cul-de-sac. Justin puts his phone in the cup holder as his gas pedal hits the floor. His car hits the driver's door perfectly, and Brock's car is shoved completely over the curb onto someone's lawn. His ear rests on his shoulder peacefully, as though he were only sleeping.

Katie: Seems like it'll be a fun night!

Justin's door is stuck. His ears are ringing. Manoeuvring around the airbag, he wriggles into the back seat and exits the opposite rear door, not closing it behind him. His fingers tear at his hair as he walks back the way he came. His jacket is only zipped halfway up.

Sandals in the snow, Justin's footprints appear for the first time on Andrea's driveway. The doorbell rings three times.

Andrea: Oh I've gotta go now! I think he's here!

She opens the door, beaming.

"Hey–"

"There's been an accident."

3rd PLACE

Tragic Love

Sarah Kirkpatrick

I arrived at work at 9:05am, as usual. As I entered the restaurant, the smell of cheap coffee, eggs and smoked bacon overtook my senses. One homely looking woman was slumped over at the bar drowning her sorrows in liquor, and a lone man sat in a large booth on the opposite side of the room staring off into the distance. All I could hear was the woman's quiet sobs as she rested her face on the mahogany bar top. It was nothing out of the ordinary; this restaurant's the kind of place people come to pity themselves.

I headed to the back to drop off my belongings. My white Vans were scuff-free and laced perfectly, my blue skirt dangled just inches above my knees. With my hair up in a messy bun, and my notepad and pencil in hand, I was ready to start my workday.

Ten minutes later, I threw the chrome kitchen doors open and re-entered the rustic dining area. The little old man was the only person still in the place. As I surveyed the dingy dining room, I wondered why I still wanted to work in this graveyard.

"Why am I here?" I muttered to myself.

I groaned as I shuffled over to the man's table. He wore a brown felt fedora, green plaid shirt, beige khakis and a pair of thick black-framed glasses. His face was droopy, wrinkles individually outlined each of his features. Atop his upper lip sat a bushy, grey moustache, and hair of the same colour leaked out of his fedora. He sat with his hands folded as he stared out the window.

"Good morning, sir." I stood there tapping my pencil on my notepad. His gaze still fixated on the passing cars. "Good morning, sir," I repeated.

"Oh! Sorry love. Didn't see ya there," he said with a chuckle.

"Can I get you anything?" I asked.

"Yes please! Two stacks of pancakes and two black coffees please, darling."

"Of course sir." I scribbled his order down onto a blank sheet. I glanced down at the table and noticed a small framed photo of a stunning young woman just in front of the man. "Who is that a photo of?" I asked.

"Oh! That's my wife." We exchanged cheeky smiles.

"Two stacks and two coffees comin' right up." I closed my notepad and walked back behind the bar. I tacked the order slip onto the pin that dangled in the kitchen window and waited.

* * * * *

"Order up!" yelled a voice from the kitchen. I walked over to the kitchen window, slid the man's tray of food onto my shoulder and carried it over to his table. As I placed the steaming stacks of pancakes and coffee in front of the man, my stomach groaned like a dying whale.

"Enjoy. Let me know if you need anything."

"Would you like to join me?" the man asked. I really wanted to say yes, but it was against store policy.

"Thank you for offering, but I'm okay." I plastered a fake smile onto my face.

"Pshhh have a seat, I don't bite," he gestured to the seat across from him. "...it's not even busy," he said as he glanced around the empty restaurant. I smiled nervously.

I flattened my skirt onto the back of my thighs as I sat down across from the man. He slid one of each item over to me.

"Are you sure?" I asked.

"Yes! Call me Dave, darling. My wife couldn't be here, and I know she'd want someone else to enjoy this meal." He smiled at her photo and caressed its frame. Man, I wish someone would look at me like that.

"Tell me about your wife," I said. I'm such a hopeless romantic, there's nothing I enjoy more than a good love story.

His eyebrows rose into high arches, the ends of his moustache perking up with excitement.

"Well, Marie Turner was her name." His cheeks flushed pink as he spoke. "We met when we were just sixteen. The very second I laid my eyes upon her, a fire started to burn within me. I knew she was the one."

My head sat atop my folded hands, and my mind fixated on the story as he proceeded to tell me how they ran away together. "It was a forbidden love..." he said.

"What do you mean?" I asked.

"Don't get me wrong, there's not a thing I'd have changed about that woman, but my parents didn't accept people of her kind." His expression dropped as his paper-thin lips curved downward.

"Her kind?" I picked up the delicate picture frame in my hands and analysed it. She had full pink lips, wavy black locks, and ice-blue eyes. The colour of her skin, black.

"Worthless, that's what my parents used to call her. They forbid me from seeing her, but I refused to comply. So I packed my bags..."

My eyes started to well with tears. I wondered how anyone could be that cruel to their child.

He described how they ran away with nowhere to go, no place to stay. They had nothing but each other. Homeless, they spent two years on the streets, two whole years. "April 23rd, 1952 was the day that changed it all," he said.

"What happened?" I asked. My body tingled with excitement.

"She made it," he said.

"What?"

"On that very day, she made it big." He told me how she'd landed the lead role in the Broadway musical, *Angel in Despair*.

"Finally someone saw the potential in that woman that I saw." His eyes glistened with euphoria.

Her big break got them off the streets, and brought them a lavish life.

"We were living our very own fairytale," he said.

As he walked me through their life together, I imagined them in their Gatsby-inspired mansion with a banana-yellow corvette and their two dogs, Benny and Albert, whom Dave was sure Marie loved more than him. He took my hand as he reminisced on all their memories together. That would usually make me really uncomfortable, considering we just met, but I felt like I'd known him forever.

His hand trembled slightly as he sipped his coffee. "We had a good run," Dave said. "She passed away five years ago..." He gripped my hand a little tighter.

"I'm so sorry..."

He took out his navy blue handkerchief and blotted a single tear off his wrinkled cheek. "Sorry, darling. I just miss her so much." He smiled at the thought of her.

I guess this is how my mom felt when dad died. I wouldn't know; I was only two when he passed away. I slid the sticky plates and table scraps to the side.

"My wife had Alzheimer's..." Dave said.

I lowered my head. I couldn't fathom the heartbreak he must have felt.

He said it started with minor memory loss, stuff like forgetting what she had for dinner the night before. Then she started to jumble her words, she couldn't speak. She had forgotten how to sing and dance, but she was still aware that these were the things she wanted to do forever.

"That's what broke her," said Dave. Tears were streaming down my face. "In less than a year, she was bedridden in the long-term care unit." She had no voice, no movement, no life.

I slid my left hand under my chin to give my right a break. Dave sat with both hands around his coffee cup. He rolled his head around from one shoulder to the other and cleared his throat.

"I was there when she took her last breath." A blank look crossed his face.

"Oh Dave..." I could feel his pain in my chest.

"She forgot how to breathe."

He rested his grief stricken face in his sweaty palms. He took a deep breath as he dried the last of his tears. I was left staring at the curvature of the wood veins that indented the table, then Dave spoke up. "Alzheimer's took my love from me... and it's going to take me too, darling."

My stomach was in my throat. My words wouldn't come out. "Wait...Dave..."

"Thank you for everything, darling, but I'd best be going now."

He stood up and smiled at me as he slid a fifty dollar bill under my hand. He took the photo of his wife, placed a gentle kiss on the glass and slid it into the left pocket of his shirt just above his heart. Without another word, he turned around and paced towards the doors. I couldn't shake myself of the shock he'd put me in. I couldn't force myself to move, I was frozen. He looked back at me and flashed me one last innocent smile, like nothing had ever happened.

"Dave!" I whispered. I couldn't bare the thought of letting that poor man go. The door squealed as he pushed it open. I blinked, and he was gone.

I stood with my head down and eyes closed, one hand clenching the fifty dollar bill, the other gripping the fabric just above my heart. My eyes shot open as I heard the door creak, followed by the sound of cars passing by.

"Dave?" I whispered hopefully. When I looked up, I saw four unfamiliar faces.

"Table for four, please," one of the voices said. Back to work I went. Dave won't remember the conversation we had that day, but I will never forget.

RUNNER UP

Sebastian's Debt

Allison Coole

He'd just robbed a bank. He let it sink in. Scruffy haired, baby faced Sebastian robbed a bank. Almost.

"The job pays great. You'll make great money with your skills." Markus had said.

Sebastian sat at the table across from Markus. Behind him were two other men. Both big, one had an upside down cross under his left eye, and the other wore a Rolex Daytona, heavy gold chains, and off brand Timberlands.

"Why do you think you're qualified for this job?" Sebastian wasn't exactly sure what the job was, but he sat up straighter and began to prattle on about his various jobs and spoke in length about his time at Fresh Co. Five minutes passed before he couldn't come up with anything else to say. The men left the room and told him to wait where he was.

Sebastian's right arm was sporadically raised, checking his watch, counting the minutes as they went. One, two, three, five, ten. What could they be discussing?

One day of this job would make Sebastian enough money to pay off his mom's radiation treatment, and within a couple more days of this work, he'd be able to pay all her debts and be able to save for a vacation to Prague; his mom had always wanted to visit. They came back out seventeen minutes later, exactly.

"You're good. Just sign the contract here," Markus pointed at a dotted line near the bottom of the paper. "And we'll be in contact within the next two days with more info."

Sebastian signed the sheet and watched the men leave, very clique-like. He just sat there for a little longer. What exactly had he gotten himself into?

It had been nearly three years since his mom got the news. Cancer, the doctors told her. She couldn't support herself financially, and the cost of medical bills were well into the thousands. He wanted to help her, so he got a job at the local Fresh Co. He thought any extra cash would help, but eventually he couldn't keep up and had been going into debt ever since.

He started looking for other work. He looked for anything that would let him make a little more. He looked for jobs that would pay him unofficially, under the table sort of work. He didn't know it would require robbing a bank, but then again, he didn't say no when they told him.

He had once before fallen in with the wrong crowd. Years ago, he had met some boys, and they convinced him it'd be thrilling to see if they could get into the school after hours, and that's what set him off. The click the locks would make when they picked them was exhilarating. The rush he could get off of it was more than any drug he could have tried.

They broke into several other places: the library, local pizza shops, relatively small places. The first time they got caught was when they tried to break into a pharmacy. They were lucky, all they got was a warning. Then they did it again. They got away with a couple more break ins, until that house.

365 Clover Street: he'd never forget that one. Jack, one of the boys in his group. beat up an elderly man who happened to be in the house. The man told them to go, that he'd call the cops. Jack didn't want to get caught. None of them wanted to, but Jack took it too far. As the group started to run, Sebastian hesitated. He took the man's landline off the receiver

and tossed it to him, saying the boy was Jack Jones. Jack was caught, along with the rest of them. They got three months in juvenile detention, Jack got a year. Through it all, Sebastian said one thing: it was the wrong crowd. It wasn't his fault. It wasn't who he was.

Now Sebastian was caught robbing a bank again, and he wouldn't run. He couldn't run, not again. He should've said no.

The bank was raided by a team of police who rushed in to take Sebastian out.

Sebastian was cuffed and dragged to a police cruiser, most of the media focusing on the scene and the hostages, but a few drawn to Sebastian's hood-covered face. All he wanted was to pay his debts, not get arrested.

The policemen started off towards the station, no rush to the drive. Sebastian had expected sirens or speed or something.

The two men began to talk. Sebastian was immediately drawn to the driver. He was wearing a Chicago Cubs hat, backwards. Cubs had a small daughter, and the passenger cop was planning a proposal for his boyfriend. He was going to ask him soon. Sebastian was glad they were out keeping the good citizens safe from people like him.

They began to argue about a hockey game. Their respective teams were playing that night. Cubs and the passenger had a rivalry. Sebastian understood that. He had a favourite baseball team: the Cubs, of course, being in Chicago. His roommate had a different one. They would always bet money when their teams faced each other. Sebastian caught a glimpse of the passenger in the rearview mirror. He had a goatee, or wanted to have one.

Their dispute covered a couple more topics then landed on forged documents, and how Goatee boy was supposed to hide them, not give them to their superior.

"You told me to hand them in, like nothing was wrong! You," Goatee yelled, pointing his finger in Cubs' face, "told me it'd be less suspicious that way."

According to Cubs, that's not what he said.

Sebastian wanted to remind them that he was there, and that this didn't really seem like procedure, but he was confused and curious. This was probably the most entertainment he'd get for a while. They should probably be charged, Sebastian thought. He'd almost robbed a bank, but they actually did something illegal.

They were just passing the hospital, the one where Doctor Hernandez sat him down and told him about his mother's diagnosis.The cops were raging at each other. It looked like Cubs had actually forgot he was driving. Sebastian didn't. He was watching everything, in the car and out. Cubs had one hand on the wheel; the other was emphasising every word he screamed. Goatee sat and stared. Sebastian was fully engaged, elbows on his knees, leaning as close to the front as he could get.

"Guys! Watch out!" Sebastian yelled.

"Shut up!" They'd both screamed at him. Unfortunately it was too late. They collided head on with a yellow Nissan, bouncing off the car and slamming into another.

The sound was memorable, to say the least. It was like the time he'd backed into a garbage bin, only much more intense.

Sebastian was okay, despite the glass shards piercing his skin. They'd taken two head on collisions, and Sebastian was in the back. He wiggled his toes and fingers successfully, felt sweat drip down the back of his neck. He wiped it off, red residue remaining on his hand.

Every movement hurt, like he'd slept wrong on every limb and bone. Cubs was blacked out, the airbag deployed, blood on the bag and his head. Goatee was awake, the skin on his head sliced, exposing the bone.

"Are you okay?" Sebastian asked. He was shaking. This was not supposed to happen.

"Call 911. No, don't. Don't call him. Don't call anyone, do you hear me?"

Sebastian nodded.

"Good. Now leave," Goatee said, staring down Cubs.

Sebastian didn't move. He didn't want to leave, he deserved prison time. The cop was glaring at Sebastian, when he wasn't glaring at Cubs. He fixed his mom's watch so it sat properly on his wrist. Sebastian began to back away.

"Are you sure you don't want me to –"

"Go! Seriously kid, leave."

Sebastian began to leave, backing away slowly, taking in the damage to the other cars. There was no way the people in the other cars could have survived. They were a mess of tangled steel and rubber.

Sebastian wanted to check, he wanted to see if anyone survived, but he was a coward.

He was leaving when he heard a sort of choking noise. Sebastian jerked around. Goatee had leaned over Cubs, blood seeping from his side of the car. Cubs was making inhuman noises. His arms were swinging, just barely though. Cubs was trying to fight, but he'd suffered badly.

Sebastian ran. He ran faster than he ever had when he saw that, watching his mom's watch glisten in the setting sun and letting the trees pine scented branches scrape across his arms as he passed.

Sebastian didn't get his debts paid off. He'd have to find another way, but on the bright side, he wasn't headed to jail.

RUNNER UP

The Golden Lady

Khloe Henderson

Ship to shore, There's nothing more,
Than a Captain's slave, I be
Ship to shore, Hear the roar
Of the saltwater inside me
Ship to shore, Away we go o'er
The endless sea
Is there nothing more,
But a pirate's life for me?

I awoke to the sound of incessant yelling. Hard footsteps moving quickly across the upper deck, inches from my face in my cramped quarters. A loud crack of lightning. Suddenly, I was very awake. Jumping from my bed, and running out the door, I was almost trampled by those running through the tight hallway.

"What's going on?" I desperately called out, my stomach tight with fear.

"She's goin' down!" someone yelled back, amidst the madness. The men continued running down the hall. I merged into the chaos, heading toward the stairs. I could taste the salt in the humid open air as I reached the ship's main deck. Loud crashes of angry water could be easily mistaken for the rush of blood in my own ears. A flash of lightning illuminated the quarter deck and Captain Vane Stronghold, a sturdy man with dark, intense eyes from years on the ocean. He stood with one hand on his sword and the other pointing as he shouted commands in his deep, coarse voice, unafraid.

"Men, about ship! Give way! Hard to starboard!" Obediently the men carried out the commands to the best of their abilities in the moonless night. Ropes tightened, the mast turned, men yelled, the ship bucked, and water burst over its side, sending barrels rolling across the deck. It was proper chaos.

"Oi, Eric! Don't jus' stand there, lend a hand." McAvoy called out and shoved a bristly rope into my heavily calloused hands. I pulled back hard with the rest of the men, unsure as to what purpose it served; my muscles protested. I was beginning to believe that this was the night I was going to die. I could vividly picture the water engulfing us, as if it had already happened. It would be over before dawn, and there was nothing we could do about it. Any action we could make in an attempt to save ourselves was utterly futile. Nevertheless, the men of the *Golden Lady* persisted. After all she had done for us, it was the least we could do. I guessed that trying to do something was better than sitting around awaiting the reaper.

What felt like hours passed, and the storm continued: relentless; merciless. The rain felt like sharp knives, and the thunder sounded like the cannon of a nearby ship. On the moonless night, our only supply of light was the frequent flash of white lighting across the sky. I was soaked to the skin in both salt water and sweat. Like all the other men on deck, I breathed heavily. Chances of survival dissipated as the boat creaked and the waves crashed.

In the moments I assumed would be my last, I thought of my family. Images of my seafaring father, mother and my dear, sweet sister distracted me from the inevitable. I wondered if this was how my father felt when the sea took him.

"I'll die in the arms of your mother or die in the arms of the sea," he would say, always adding, with a look I didn't quite understand at my young age, "I hope it is the sea, boy, then I won't have to watch the sadness in her eyes, one more time, as I leave her. A life at sea is not meant for a husband or a father, boy, I've learned that the hard way. When you're at sea, you miss home and when you are home, you miss the sea. It tears a man apart. You can't have both."

That was the last piece of advice my dear father gave me – you can't have both. After my father was taken from us, it was just us three. My mother and sister became the brightest lights of my life; I couldn't both care for them and have a love of my own, and that was fine. I was their provider, their protector, the one who loved them most. Everything I ever did, I did for them; robbing the rich for money to buy food, working four jobs and caring for the family cow to sell cheese and milk to keep a roof over our heads. I dreamt of a day when we would have enough money to leave our decrepit village and, together, sail across to a better place. The ocean was going to be the passage to a new life.

When they both became sick and died, far too young, I sold the cow, burned down our old wooden shack and, with nothing to keep me home, a life at sea was the sole choice. I jumped on a ship, toward a new beginning. The sea had been my home ever since, and after all this time it was as if the ocean and I had become one. I set sail and never planned to step on dry land again; where my mother and sister failed to exist, ne'er too, would I. Not once did I believe I would meet a premature death at the hand of the sea that was supposed to be my saviour. I had pictured something more heroic, perhaps something along the lines of a cannon battle with other pirates or maybe a fatal run-in with the legendary Kraken.

The shouts of the men brought me out of my thoughts and back to reality; the ship violently rocked us without mercy. The Captain had joined the men on the deck, heaving ropes with a clenched jaw. A wave crashed over the side of the boat, and a loud crack signalled the end of the mainsail which, unceremoniously, fell across the deck as men jumped out of the way. Before any action could be taken, a tidal wave engulfed the ship, swallowing the remainder of the *Golden Lady* with the intent of bringing her down to a watery grave.

I didn't want to die. In what I assumed to be my last moments, I called out to the ocean, my saviour, and declared my love and devotion to it. I begged for it to have mercy on my soul. I held my breath as everything went dark.

I awoke to the sun beating down on my eyelids, causing them to turn red. My first thought was that I had died, then I opened my eyes and tried to get my bearings. I was floating in the middle of the ocean, clinging to a scrap of wood, my shirt ripped to shreds. The salt stung my eyes as I bobbed in place, clouding my vision. My muscles ached deeply, and dried blood was caked around a cut on my arm. The wound burned in the salt water. I surveyed the horizon, but I couldn't see any other men from the ship. I could have been bobbing for days, unconscious. A dreadful thought came to me, one of suffering a slow death of starvation and dehydration in the middle of the sea. I wailed into the nothingness, all hope lost.

Hours passed. The lap of calm waves on my skin was somewhat melodic. The sun was hot on my head, so when I saw something moving beneath me in the water, I thought heatstroke was causing me to imagine things. When it brushed past my leg, I knew it was real. I knew I didn't want to be killed by a shark! I scrambled onto the top of the wooden plank. Lying on my stomach, I peered over the edge of the wood and spotted a fin dart beneath me.

Then, beneath the surface, a face moving up toward me; at first, a terrible, horrible thought told me it was the remains of a shipmate, but, it was far too beautiful to be a corpse. It was a lady with large, deep blue eyes and long, golden, hair cascading around her and framing her face. Turquoise scales covered the otherworldly tail that swirled below her. She pushed out of the water, laid her hands on both sides of my face, and she kissed me.

Suddenly, I couldn't breathe and began to panic. It was like someone had clapped a pillow over my mouth and nose; my neck began to itch and I couldn't move my legs. Taking my face in her hands, she pulled me, gently, into the water, her golden tresses enveloping me all the while. I let myself slip off the wooden scrap into her embrace. Once underwater, I opened my eyes, and they no longer burned. My arm no longer bled, and I no longer felt like I couldn't breathe. I looked closer at the lady, her piercing blue eyes, her golden mane and her magnificent blue scaled tail. I looked at myself and, to my astonishment, I too had a scaled tail, green in colour.

This magnificent golden lady, my saviour, held her hand out to me, and I took it.

RUNNER UP

My Little Piece of Heaven

Jodie Quinton

The lights are off, save for the little Christmas lights hanging above me. The red and green hues twinkle in the dark and cast shadows down my spine and the binding of those around me.

I study the room that lies before me, as I did yesterday, and the day before that, and the day before that. It hardly changes. Things are moved around and thrown to new spots. But they're the same things, and they're placed by the same person. I know my place, as he knows his, and she knows hers.

The smell of dust and aged pages surround my every waking moment. It carries me into a trance of complete blissfulness.

As I bathe in the aroma, the lights hanging from the white ceiling flash on above me, overpowering the dim glow of the Christmas lights lining the shelves.

A tall, pale girl walks into the bedroom. Her eyes are the colour of the sky before a storm. They pierce through the room like freshly sharpened daggers. Her blonde hair hangs over her face, swishing forward as she places her brown, worn out slippers beside the shoe shelves that hug the corner of her cherry blossom pink bedroom. She slowly stands up and subconsciously pushes a strand of hair behind her ear.

She steps forwards towards her dresser. The top of it is covered with knick-knacks and unimportant things that have found a home there. Mirrors, candles, papers, chalk: they clutter the table. Speakers lie at either end, connecting to the outlet hiding behind the long black and white bench that is placed beneath the picturesque window. The frame is slightly ajar, and a breeze creeps through the opening, spilling into the room. The taste of morning dew and spring cedar fills me, and I feel refreshed.

The rising sun begins to brighten the room even further, minute after minute, pouring in and setting the room ablaze. The wall across from the window illuminates from the attention of the rays. Rows of painting, both bought and made, line the walls. One after the other, each depicts scenes of glorious wars or warm winter nights in the woods. I can feel my heart pulling out of my chest toward the images.

Their cool tones and bright splats of colour battle with one another in a never-ending fight for control of the space. The scent of the paint finish cuts through the air like an arrow cutting through the flesh of an innocent child.

The creek of footsteps on the wooden floor grabs my attention, and I look up to see the girl walking towards me. She crawls onto her bed, and the mattress curves around her as if it is embracing her presence. The freshly pressed white sheets begin to wrinkle as she throws her matching pillows to the side to get closer to me.

She raises her hand and brushes her long, soft fingertips across our spines. Her eyes scan us back and forth in a hypnotising trance. The gears of her mind grinding against each other, questioning which one of us she'll choose today.

My heart pounds faster and faster. I can almost hear it, like the faint pounding of a drum in my ears. My pages curl with anticipation each time she glances in my direction. The world begins to spin, and I feel as if the shelf above me is caving in, trying to suffocate me.

Then, all of a sudden, her gaze rests on me, giving off a warmth stronger than the sun pouring in through the window. An eternity passes before she finally reaches out and pulls me off of my all too familiar shelf. The others groan with jealousy, but I don't care. All I can focus on is her smile, which is as wide as it was the first time she laid eyes on me all those months ago.

Her warm hands radiate through me, elating every sense as my heart vibrates through my chest with ecstasy. She sits down in the centre of her bed, crossing her legs on top of one another and places me gently to her right. I look up to see the endless rows of my friends: some new, some old, some waiting to be chosen, some already chosen dozens of times before. Their colours create rows of rainbows spanning the length of the wall. A beautiful mirage of hours spent watching her read them one by one. Waiting jealousy for her to reach my name on her ever growing list. And finally, after all those moths of waiting, she chooses me.

The girl picks up a metallic mug filled with Earl Grey tea that has been steeping for several minutes. The steam rises up and travels towards me, carrying the scent of serenity and disappearing into the air like the fleeting wisps of smoke from an old pipe. She takes a long sip and sighs, placing the mug back onto one of the lower shelves of the black headboard that I have lived on for the past several months.

She reaches over to me and places me on her lap. Her eyes scan my cover, searching for the meaning in my title as if it would answer all of the questions that philosophers have been asking for centuries. She opens up my cover, making sense of the little, horizontal scribbles that cover my body and transforming them into a story of utmost joy and suffering. Her warm hands run along my pages, making me shiver with the delight of being so close to someone who loves me with such a deep, unyielding passion. As she reads, I watch the sun slowly continue to rise over the treetops, and I melt into her lap, knowing that I will always find a home in this room, in this little piece of heaven.

RUNNER UP

Mirror

Holly Ann Lavergne

Truth.

Always given, but not always received.

I watch, have always watched, regardless of whether she'd like to be seen.

A young girl awakens me and I stay with her, faithfully.

Each day looking, not always seeing. Bright blue eyes began, lilted like a feather of honey and sweet like syrup. At first a small room, with speckled corners and flowered spreads. She placed her hand upon me, searching. Realising. Poppy collar, ruffled hem. She twirled, awed by the folds of plaid sweeping her sides. Flying like a bird, she grew, quickly in sureness, in awareness. She liked to sit, day after day, with little china girls and pots, alone but for her chatter. And she laughed, trembling my surface like a glass pond.

Separated again and again by flashes and darkness, comings and goings. I always see, and I always reflect.

Close up, she brushes, sprays, pinches, stares. Tufts of powder glinting in the light. Coral pressed and outlined. Rouge lips, close to me, pressed together in colour. Admiration and glee smudged across her cheeks. She steps into a dress, one I've watched being sewn, over evenings and into nights. After poring over letters and smiling in the dark. While swinging her shoulders like tomorrow was already here. Red sleeved gown, hugging her waist and drifting down her thighs. Embroidered blossoms that climbed pleats and glowed in her eyes. I showed her what she imagined: a heart seeing, feeling, and knowing what it wanted.

Still a young girl. Rushing off to meet crowds, to dance unseen by me into the night. Seen by someone else.

And then gone was the pink room, dappled with growth and glee. A girl in white emerged, untouched by colour. Stark. A bun of unknotted hair. Only glimpses, no longer stares. Reflections in window, of trains, of dormitories. In the eyes of children losing something she still had. Yet, something they were all losing. Glints in the medals of soldiers, in the blood trickling to the floor and staining locks of honey. Hardening and touching within, what was untouched.

Still. A young girl.

And then happiness. Leaning over a bridge clasping his hand and watching the fish swim about, yet also seeing herself anew, seeing me. It was not always that she really looked or really saw. He looked too, but did not see.

Separated by darkness. A long time passed, and I did not see her. We met again in a cold, small room. Grey and stained, with a small bed and chair. No blossoms to climb, nothing to be climbed. She was no longer alone, however she felt it, and she looked into me through a brewing fog. A baby lay crying in her arms, yet no one came to help. She lay down too, sealed from not only herself but from me. Sobbing tears of guilt and regret, for herself and for him. The baby looked at me, and I reflected back what I saw. Mirrored in her eyes was herself; hope brewed unknown in those streams, trickling down their faces.

Replacing the darkness was a pair of girls. The days never ceased to come and go, over and over. A young girl, just realising; a rising one, just living. In a yellow hall brimming with frames of gold, encasing beams of pride, they sat together. I reflected truthfully, like always, the chatter and the embraces. They talked and hugged and left hand in hand. Crying of joy this time. But when she returned, my girl who I'd watched all along, was no longer part of a pair.

Snapshots filled the wall opposite me. The one I watched often, as she left each morning and returned each night, worn with work. Captured not by me and my reflection, my smooth surface, my reality. Captured by a lens, by a heart, not by truth. What she sees is not always what I reflect, and what she captures is not always what I see. Yet they showed moments of sparkling smiles, ones that I had seen radiated in a young girl years ago. And I saw her light up again, just seeing those photos of her little one, growing and learning, succeeding and loving.

She was no longer a young girl, but she carried that girl too.

Her honey faded, and her feathers fell. Her porcelain face drooped and wrinkled, but often into a grin. Slate coloured strands fell around her bright eyes, unfaded by age. Untamed even after all those years of seeing, of feeling. She rocked in front of the window with a ball of coloured wool, creating once more. I watch her and feel important, as she looks through me with a twinkle in her eyes that is even brighter than before. Lengths settle on her knees, resting in the weathering chair that always faces her window. A view of blossoms and vines frame the window, encasing me. I see her winding a piece, a strand of blue wool dancing around her finger.

Then: excitement. Months of waiting and seeing. My girl rests her hand on her daughter, jumping and giggling as she feels something. Life. Each day passes faster than the last, like she was waiting for this moment.

Finally she holds him in her arms, tears falling once more. Photos are snapping; her daughter is hugging her. They stand in a grand room, paintings adorning the walls and fruit piling in bowls. But it is not the vastness of the room that they see or the clear reflection I project. They look past it and see me, see themselves. Mirrored in me are three unmisted figures, rocking into a world where I cannot follow, but can only show: the truth.

RUNNER UP

The Start of the Show

Paula Turnbull

I stand back and breathe in the the different scents that mingle to create the perfume that I call life. There's the sharp stale smell of sweat, the bittersweet wave of obnoxious floral perfume, wet paint drying, and coffee grounds. I don't know where to look because everything is such a frenzy of activity. All around me, workers are scurrying back and forth, trying to appease everyone's needs, like an army of rats. The lights above my head are fairly dim, and barely illuminate the backstage area, a place that I am about to become very familiar with.

This wasn't how I wanted to start my big debut. I pictured myself graduating high school and simply stepping out into the workforce. Heck, I was expecting a handwritten invitation to perform. That was before I got my feet grounded in reality and realised that if I wanted to get myself into show business, I would have to start at the bottom of the pack. Maybe even below that.

I know at this point, you're probably a bit confused, and thinking, "Wait. Why not go to school?"

Or maybe even... "Who even are you, and why am I reading this"?

Well let me answer both of those questions. My name is Kelsey. I'm average height with dull grey eyes and mousy hair that's a boring mud brown. I feel like I blend in anywhere, as

I'm hardly recognisable. And yet, that all changes when I am on the stage.

I'm sure that you're all thinking, Wow. Is she ever vain and full of herself. But for me, acting is where I belong. It's where I excel at something. Memories slip away and moments blend together until I'm just a character in the spotlight.

I didn't have the best beginning. My mom left when I was five, leaving my dad to raise three kids while he struggled to make ends meet. This is how I landed myself in the position I'm in now. With not enough money to go to college to pursue my love of theatre, and no connections, I decided to take matters into my own hands, and start an internship with the theatre downtown. Okay, so it wasn't an internship, it was volunteering. I know that I should have gotten a job first. But I believed that if I just started somewhere, things would begin to fall in line.

"Well!"

A loud and booming voice startles me into the present. I jump in surprise, being so clearly lost in my thoughts that I didn't notice that life was still going on without me.

"Are you just going to stand there and let in the heat, or are you going to get to work?"

I'm about to laugh and protest that it's even warmer inside the theatre, when I glance up and reconsider. Standing before me is the most intimidating man I've ever seen. At the towering statue of 4'3", he's the epitome of terrifying. He has cold, black eyes, and frown lines that cause his face to seem like he's perpetually glaring. His big shaggy eyebrows are knit together into a frown, which startlingly contrasts with his completely bald head. I immediately know that he means business, not pleasure.

"Ummm," I stutter tentatively. Apparently my ability to string together sentences has vanished as much as his hairline.

"I'm new. What –"

"No kidding," he snaps. "I can see that. Well. Why are you standing there. Get going, and stop yammering". Still slightly confused and frightened by his brief and startling nature, I rush inside. Unfortunately for me, this means that I'm not paying attention to where I'm going.

I rush forward at full speed and collide with a very large cart that's filled costumes. It careens over and, much to my dismay, leotards fly in every direction.

As I watch random hats, boas, and what appears to be a pair of underwear go sailing past my head, in an utterly surreal display of grace, I take a wobbling step forward to save them. However, in my haste, I fail to notice a very slippery pair of women's tights. I go down hard, crashing into the middle of the heap, bearing a very close resemblance to a moulting flamingo attempting to do yoga. I attempt to get up without looking like a beluga whale caught in a fishing net, but quickly realise that I'm stuck. It was then that I look up and see that I've attracted an audience.

"Need any help?" a deep voice rumbles, cutting through the laughter that has already begun. I accept the hand that's offered and try to hide my face, my cheeks blushing a darker shade of crimson. I peek out of the corner of my eye, and catch sight of a jovial looking man in his early thirties with a round face, bald head, and kind eyes. I bend over and attempt to pick up the mess that I created, hoping that no one else mentions my embarrassing fate.

"I'm so sorry. I —-" I start to say, but he cuts me off.

"Don't worry about it. This happens to everyone some time or other. It occurs so often that I call it 'the laundry heap'." I begin to feel a bit better, but my humiliation is still fresh. Thankfully, the gathered crowd is dissipating, although I'm sure the stage hands will be commenting on my disaster for weeks to come.

The man slowly kneels down to help me, and I can tell by the stiff crackle of his joints that this isn't the easiest thing for him to do.

"I'm Phil, by the way," he announces, as he reaches for a pile of lace frocks and begins to straighten them. "I can't help but notice that your first day may be a hard one."

I begin to agree with what he's saying, but quickly worry that I may appear to be rude, and stop short, mid-nod.

"Well, my first day wasn't easy either," he begins. "I mean, I was hired to do tech, but ended up getting stuck in costumes. Apparently I have a natural aptitude to find what looks good on people and —-" he stops short, and pulls out a huge straw hat with feathers on the brim, "– this would look incredible on you. It's what the star was supposed to wear. But she quit last minute. Something about not enough green skittles in her candy dish."

He unceremoniously plunks the hat on my head. He then takes a delicate scarf and wraps it around my shoulders. I'm beginning to feel like a feather duster combined with a carpet until he says, "Done," and pulls out a mirror. The materials shouldn't go together, and yet, it looks like they were made for each other.

"The master has done his work again!" he announces in a theatrical voice. "From damsel in distress to damsel in the dress. You look like a piece of art."

I step back and glance in the mirror, only to gasp in surprise. The colours on the hat heighten the rosy hues of pink in my cheeks, and the intricate wrap on he scarf makes me look like a princess from far away. I barely even recognise myself.

Yet again, my illusion of glamour is shattered as a very familiar voice startles me. Even though my back is to him, I feel a tingle beginning to spread through my back. It's the man that yelled at me for standing near the door. My mind immediately jumps to the thought of losing my chance to be near a stage, of being fired. I start to freeze up.

"What are you doing here!" he demands.

I try to answer, but I can't move. I am paralysed with fear.

"You need to be onstage now."

He doesn't recognise me, I think, relieved.

Phil notices the situation, and improvises. "We just had some costume changes, but Daria is on her way." I'm about to ask who Daria is, but Phil whispers, "Roll with it," and pushes me towards the stage door.

Just before I enter, Phil snags my sleeve. He speaks hurriedly, and his words blur together.

"After the lead quit, we were looking for a new face. Daria got chosen for an audition, but she didn't show up. Thankfully, you were mistaken for her, so go out there."

"But..." I protest.

"You were born for theatre, I can see it in you," Phil replies. "Now take the stage, and give it your all."

He opens the door, and I stumble out onstage. The stage light wraps around me like a warm, comforting blanket, and I know that this is where I belong. This is the moment I've been waiting for. This is my chance. I will succeed.

GRADES 9 - 10

1st PLACE

I Exist (Past, Present and Future)

Aluki Chupik-Hall

The earth stalls, juts under me, and catapults me into what I'm not entirely ready for. Under the beast I ride, metal hits the yellow line, oh, how it hits. Wheels shouldn't know how to kiss the ground. Tires should hit the road, do all the dirty work, but wheels shouldn't be bare, skin against skin. When tire rubber breaks, that summer night becomes pregnant full of problems.

But I suppose I'm being dramatic.

I get out. I slam the door. It doesn't ring out. It dissipates into the empty sky. The worst kind of revenge is the insignificant kind. So, I examine the issue. The tire is flat against the ground, and there's nothing I can do to fix it. I curse the fact that I never learned to change a tire. I remember the exact moment in my life when my father presented me the opportunity to learn. I hated my father. Thus, by association, I hated changing tires.

My phone rings in my car. The screen lights up like a search beacon in the empty sky. Defeated, I slide into the passenger seat to check it. It's my girlfriend. I left the previous texts unread, the ones about this being my last chance, and that I better not blow it. I ignored them because I thought I'd be at her parent's house party by now, with real feelings and a kiss.

I guess I blew that too. My love life hit the road, flipped, and fell in the ditch. My car has a flat tire.

I bury my head in my hands as the rest of the texts come flooding in, about how I wasn't there yet, and how I couldn't even be trusted with a simple evening. I swear at myself with my nose pressing against the dash. I cry. Then, I pick up my phone, and when I should call my girlfriend, I call a towing company. I let her wonder where I'm gone to. She probably thinks I'm still at home, forgetting about her. But this time, I made an effort, really made an effort, and the universe just doesn't want it to happen.

I get out of the car again. I stand over the ditch, my feet inches from falling over the edge. Cars whip past. The earth is sullen, slow. The world isn't listening. I yell anything I want. Strings of words come out, long-winded sentences that only I can understand. That only I need to understand.

"I exist," I say to the unresponsive landscape. My throat burns, but for some reason, I say it. It's funny how with nobody around we still feel the need to justify our place in the world.

There is a blinding light. I wave my hands, and the yellow tow truck pulls up beside me. It parks, and a man steps out to see me, huddled beside my burst tire like I've made it a home. He takes a look at the car and says something in a language made up of grunts and murmurs, so I take my phone and sit in the ditch as he hooks up the car.

There are seven missed calls from my girlfriend. I return them.

"Hey." My voice still hurts.

"What were you thinking? Where are you?"

"My car got a flat tire. I'm getting towed."

There's nothing. Well, not nothing. There's the sound of the air coming through from her side, and it's bloated with emotion, crackling and warm. There's the sound of the crane clambering against my car. There's the sound of the oven opening and closing, the warmth of her kitchen, her mother's footsteps. Her meekness. Mine. The wide, crushing breadth of the earth between us. There's never nothing, I suppose.

"Don't bother coming here, then. We're through," she says.

"Because my car broke down?" I ask.

"Because of everything, okay?"

"Okay," I say, and hang up. I don't know if she wanted to continue the conversation. I didn't want to. Maybe it's a good thing I never learned to change a tire, I think.

My car is hooked up. The man offers me a seat beside him while my car drags behind.

"Where to?" he asks, and I tell him. We drive away from that spot on the highway, until I can't see it, or even recall what it looked like. Maybe I'll drive past it a million more times. Maybe never. I'll see a million pictures of me standing next to her, or none. But those things remain lodged in the past, impossible to retrieve, to recreate.

The yellow line stretches on, and the past becomes visible only in the rearview mirror, closer than it appears, and perpetually impossible to touch by moving forwards.

2nd PLACE

Driving with no Destination

Julia Llewellyn

My pale blue 1969 Dodge Charger had its windows down all the way, and my left arm was dangling out the window. It was sunny and warm, and the radio played in the background. I was driving with no particular destination. I suppose I liked to drive, simply to be able to roll my windows down and let my hair whip around in the wind. I usually ended up at a beach or diner, sometimes both if I had the time. But those weren't the peaks of my journey.

The car was my prized possession; I kept it clean, and before he died, my grandpa was teaching me how to maintain it. It was his car, and he left it to me in his will. My mother told me it was a waste of money, and to focus on something that wasn't more than twice as old as I was. She didn't understand.

I turned my head and spotted the beach. It was the one I came to regularly. The sand was white, and the water was clear. There were a few large rocks you could perch on to watch the sunset and an ice cream stand not far away from the beach. My wallet was on the dash, and I could already taste the ice cream. Mint chocolate chip was my favourite. The stand was close, and my music was loud.

"Don't you… forget about me…"

I smiled and sang along.

"As you walk on by…"

As I pulled up to the ice cream stand, I turned the radio down but left the car running. I wouldn't be long.

I walked up to the stand and scanned the list of flavours, though I already knew what I wanted, so I let my eyes flit towards the picnic tables beside the stand as I waited for someone to come to the window and take my order. It was not a popular spot, only a few other people were there. I turned my gaze upon the table closest to me and a brown haired boy met my eyes. I felt myself draw in a breath as I waited for him to break eye contact.

"Excuse me."

I quickly turned back to the window. In front of me was a girl, picking at her nails as if she was bored.

"Hi. Sorry," I apologised.

She shrugged. "What can I get you?" she asked.

"Um, can I get a mint chip cone please? Two scoops."

The girl nodded and went farther back into the shop. I watched her pull a cone from a cardboard case that was attached to the wall (I hoped it wouldn't be stale), before casually turning my gaze back onto the table. The boy was watching me, and he smirked as our eyes met again. Then he got up, and I watched him walk off towards the parking lot. I forced my eyes back to the window, where the girl was holding out the cone.

"That'll be three seventy-five," she said, staring down at her nails again. I smiled, forgetting about the boy for a moment and handed her the money.

I made my way back to my car, turned the radio back up and pulled out onto the street. I licked the drips from my ice cream as I drove to the beach, sighing as they hit my tongue. They were cold and minty.

As I wandered down the sandy beach, my Toms dangled from my fingers. The white sand was squishy and soft beneath my toes. The summer breeze warmed my body. The sun was setting so I made a beeline for the large boulders, but as I approached them, I noticed a silhouette perched on top of the boulder. It was him. My steps faltered. He didn't notice me approach. Instead, he licked his ice cream and stared out at the setting sun. I blew out a harsh breath and kept walking towards the boulders. They didn't belong to him.

I pulled myself onto the boulder, using the familiar grooves and the small rocks to assist me. I had performed this trick with only one hand many times.

The boy was startled as I sat myself down beside him. His eyes grew wide with surprise and he almost dropped his ice cream.

"Jeez, if you're going to sit on my boulder, you could at least announce yourself," he said. Then he broke out into a big grin. "You're that girl who was staring at me at the ice cream stand."

I frowned. "No, you were staring at me." I contradicted. He shook his head.

"I specifically remember you staring at me. Hey, did you follow me here?" he teased.

"No." I said, giving him a cold look. "I come here all the time."

He smiled. "Well I'm sorry, I'm just not used to strange girls approaching me on the beach and sitting on my boulder," he said. I opened my mouth but he kept talking. "I'm Jonah."

I gave him a questioning look. "You're strange, Jonah," I told him after a moment.

He shook his head. "No, just Jonah," he said, cheekily.

I rolled my eyes but couldn't hold back my smile. "I'm Jane," I told him.

He nodded, taking another lick of his ice cream. He was down to the cone.

We sat there in silence, eating our ice cream and staring out across the water. The small waves lapped up against the sand of the beach. It looked so calm, and the reflection of the sunset on the water gave it a pink-orange tinge.

"So what's a pretty girl like you doing out here all alone on a Friday night?" Jonah asked me, taking a bite of his cone. He chewed it as he watched a slow blush creep onto my cheeks. He called me pretty.

"Well, I wanted to come see the sunset I suppose. I didn't really come here on purpose," I admitted. Jonah turned to face me and I mirrored his actions.

"You simply drove here? By accident?" he questioned.

I thought about it for a moment, then nodded. "Yeah I guess I did."

Jonah laughed quietly. "I like you Jane," he said. I blushed again.

"Um, thanks."

Jonah took the last bite of his ice cream cone and then slid off of the rock. "Want to take a walk?" he asked, and I smiled.

"Sure."

Jonah held out his hand to me and I took it, sliding off the rock myself. I licked my ice cream again, nearing the cone.

"So what do you like to do, Jane?" he asked me.

I smiled as I bent over to grab my shoes. "I like long walks on the beach, I suppose," I said, and he laughed.

We neared the waves and my feet sunk into the wet sand. It was cold, but not unpleasantly so. I took a bite of my cone.

"What do you like to do, Jonah?" I asked him, feeling myself relax.

He looked up at the sky and stroked his chin, pretending to think. "I guess I like long walks on the beach too. And I like eating ice cream."

We neared where I had parked my car, and I noticed another car father away in the parking lot for the first time. I chewed on the last of my cone, before slipping my shoes back on. My toes were sandy, but I didn't mind very much.

"Is that your car?" Jonah asked, gesturing to it. I nodded.

"Is that yours?" I questioned, pointing to the one father away from us.

"Yeah. I like old cars," he told me.

I smiled. "Me too! Mines a '69 Dodge Charger," I told him, my smile growing wide as we approached my car.

Jonah's eyes scanned the car. "The colour is really cool. Mine's just black," he said.

"I like it because it's different. Kind of like me," I confessed.

Jonah smiled, walking around the car and examining the windows. "I'm different too. I also have to go."

I watched Jonah walk towards his car, before getting in my own. I put the key in the ignition and the radio turned on.

"I'll see you around!" I heard him call as he opened his door.

"Bye!" I yelled back.

As I pulled out of the lot, I smiled. It seemed as if with Jonah, I finally had a destination.

3rd PLACE

The Moon's Light

Kendra Chalut

Everyone in my town knew of the stories about the mythical figures that would come and take you away if you strayed too far off of the path on the farm's property. But that wouldn't stop me.

I've been investigating this place for a couple of years, trying to figure out if these beings really existed or if someone was out there, kidnapping people and taking them elsewhere. Personally, I never believed the rumours, but people started disappearing more frequently a year after I moved to this nobody town.

There were tales about beings that would come out of the lake near the farm, but that didn't make sense. People can't breathe underwater. Others said that when fog surrounded the woods the beings would come from the trees and whisk you away. That made more sense than the lake thing, but why would they take you into the woods?

Now as I stood atop the hill overlooking the property, anyone could see how beautiful the farm actually was. The sound of the water on the edge of the property echoed around it and sounded like a beautiful song with the sound of the trees and their leaves swishing around in the wind.

Taking a deep breath I pulled out one of the cameras I had brought with me. I pointed it at the lake and set it up to record. Throwing my bag back over my shoulder I continued down the hill towards the path in front of the woods.

The wind whistled, and the moon shone down, turning the ground beneath me silver and white.

The trees were draped in shadows and fair shimmering light, both caused by the position of the moon. I crouched and put my bag back down on the ground and pulled out another camera.

The world went silent for a moment, and I looked around. There was still wind; the trees were moving like before, but now it was silent.

Who are you?

I jumped a little as the sound of the wind came roaring back with the sound of the leaves, and I stumbled, landing on my butt. Bracing myself with my arms I looked around. There was no one there.

"Hey! If anyone's there, come on out!"

There was no response to my call, just the wind whipping through the leaves.

I nervously grabbed the camera, putting it back into position and setting it to record, putting another facing the other direction. I needed to cover as much of the woods as I could.

I stood up and looked around, despite the moon's light, there were still dark spaces where someone could be lurking. I stuck my hand into my bag and rooted around for the small flashlight I'd brought. I found it and clicked on the button.

I turned my attention to the darker corner of the barn. In the corner was a crow or raven, which shot into the air and let out an angry caw.

I held back a nervous laugh. Those stories are fake, calm down! They're not real. I crossed my arms, grumbling at myself before grabbing my bag and walking to the edge of the water.

The view was breathtaking. The way the moon turned the deep blue-water silver with its light was glorious. The little waves crashed and crumbled, dying away to nothing beside my feet.

I felt as if I could stare into the water forever.

I shook my head. Not the time!

I set my bag farther away from the waterline to make sure that the cameras didn't get wet and pulled one out. I set them up along the edge of the water.

A stone sparkling caught my eye, and I rooted it out of the ground. When I pulled it out, I felt a breath on my neck, and I let out a shriek and fell back, the water washing over me, soaking my clothes.

I was breathing heavily and scrambled to my feet looking around the lit up area. The moon's glow seemed to bring my attention to the woods. Just as my eyes laid on the dark twisting trees a twig snapped. I whipped away from the trees and clutched the flashlight, turning it so fast towards the source of the sound I almost dropped it.

Look at me...

My whole body shivered and the feeling of dread was indescribable. I was frozen, and it felt as if my body moved on its own as I turned and faced the woods.

The fog had rolled off of the lake and had started to cover the ground, it lifted as a draft of wind grabbed it, blocking my view and blinding me.

I'm here...

I turned and waved my hand trying to dispel the fog, and to my surprise, it was gone. There, among the dark twisting trunk, illuminated by the moon stood the tall human-like figure.

I let out a gasp. "H-Hey! How long have you been there?" I called out my question and started to consider the sweat on my forehead.

I've been waiting...

I fiddled with my fingers nervously. This being looked like an angel; it was clothed in long white robes and had pale skin. Its hair was hidden from view by a hood that nearly covered its golden eyes. There was a strange aura around this thing, and I was puzzled.

"Who are you?" I whispered, looking at it with tense shoulders.

I am what you seek.

What do I seek? What is... my internal thought trailed off. This is the thing taking people away. The stories were true. My heart started pounding.

I turned to run but I was frozen, shaking now as it looked at me.

Come, it said without moving its mouth. You need the answers.

It swayed softly before extending a long, thin arm and waving away the thick tangles of the woods.

Come, we have little time.

I gazed at it. It wanted me to come, there was something weird, some feeling compelling me to join this thing. I didn't want to, but my legs started moving heavily and clumsily towards this angel.

I was still shaking when I got closer to it. I could see now that it had sharp features in its face and its eyes were blank and meaningless. It extended a hand to me and smiled softly.

It's okay... Come... They will wait.

I looked at it and with a shaking voice spoke again. "Who?" it came clearer than I thought.

I cannot explain here. We've only a few moments.

Its voice was hurried, and it gave me a sense of urgency. I glanced at its hand; it was soft-looking with no dents or scars.

Or remnants of mud, I thought, as I whipped my filthy hand on my dirty pants. I reached out and took its hand.

It wasn't as soft as it looked, almost jagged. I looked up and the soft pleasant smile had twisted in some way as the grip on my hand grew stronger almost as if a clamp was holding me.

Dread swept over me but a soothing voice coming from in front of me soothed the worry.

Fear not child, you're protected by my will and will survive the journey. Now, take a deep breath and close your eyes...

I took a deep breath as instructed and closed my eyes. As soon as I did the odd calming feeling faded; fear, dread, and worry swept over me.

In an instant, I was gone.

The cameras were rolling. The film held nothing but the screams of a human from the fog. The fog that blocked the sight of any who were near and stopped the truth from being told.

As the cameras sat unmoving, a sound swept through the property. The screens cracked and the tape burned. Any evidence of what had happened was gone.

From atop the hill on the beautiful farm property, the fog cleared, crawling back to the water and sliding along the silver streaks from the moon.

The trees were covered in shadows of silver, twisting and swirling together in a graceful shape before the silver of the moon slid across the ground and returned to the lake.

Upon striking the water the silver light of the moon was swept back to the middle of the water. The shadows lurched and grew, falling faster and faster to the edge of the water where the remnants of the silver light drew back. They twisted into the sky in an odd contorting display as it climbed towards the moon.

This night, another joined those who had become a part of the moon's light. They would come again to this world one day, to deliver others.

RUNNER UP

Gone Fishin'

Penelope Duran

The day was sunny and allowed his memories to flourish. His calloused hands brushed against the corrugated door, as he walked out of the old tool shed with his fishing rod and tackle. As he wiped the sweat off of his face with his mud-stained sleeve, he dashed into the plain one-story house and came back out with a cooler. He stowed his supplies in back of the aged red truck parked out front, its vanity plate glittering in the sun, even though some of the paint had worn away from the letters. Getting in the truck, he focused only on the wiry road in front of him, which had become so familiar over the years.

When he arrived at the lake he unloaded his gear onto the dock, and sat down under the canopy of trees. Droplets from the recent rain dripped from the branches onto his thinning hair. He looked at the tiny pools and was reminded of how he and Opa, his grandfather, used to fish in the rain. As his fishing line sunk into the shimmering waters, his mind drifted. He allowed his thoughts to swim as deep as they could go, back, way back, too far back to the old tales of "the magic fish" about which his Opa used to tell.

"Why do people fish for fun, if they can get fish from the store?" he had asked when he was a little too young to understand these sorts of pastimes; he wanted to play more than he wanted to fish.

"Magic," Opa said with certainty.

"Magic?"

"Haven't heard of magic fish?" Opa asked, the accent of his home country becoming more prominent as he prepared to tell a story.

"No."

"People say that there are magic fish in this lake, and if you find one, you can wish for anything."

"Anything?"

"Yes, anything. Happiness, success, *Geld*."

His grandson smiled not only at the idea that there was magic in the lake but also at the way Opa would use a German word whenever he couldn't remember the English word.

They spent so many hours looking for magic that their skin was the color of salmon. Catching fish was more important than catching a burn. They talked about magic and wished for what they each hoped. When he had asked Opa, he could see the desperate longing in his grandfather's eyes. Opa said he had everything he needed. When Opa asked his grandson what he wanted, the boy replied without hesitation.

"I don't ever want to grow up. I want days like today to last forever."

"Oh, *mein Lieber*, I want that too. But most things don't last forever."

"Then, I'd wish to be like you when I grow up."

Opa smiled. They both dipped their feet into the water. Opa taught him how to fish.

He heard a tree branch drop into the water and was shaken from his memories. The sun and blanket of humidity were making his mind sluggish. He got up, opened the cooler and pulled out a can of soda. He was about to take a sip before he paused to check the label.

Oma, his grandmother, had packed their lunches with absolute care, but Opa was insistent on taking inventory to ensure she had made no grave mistake. He asked for his grandson to check the cooler.

"Come here *mein Lieber*," Opa said, as he moved some bait into a smaller bucket.

"Yes, Opa?"

"Open up the cooler and check if the soda pop has cane sugar."

His grandson hurried to the cooler and came back with a can.

"And?"

"No cane sugar; just syrup."

"Well, we have no need for that. We'll have to remind Oma that proper provisions include soda with cane sugar and not syrup."

"What's wrong with syrup? And what's so great about cane sugar?" he asked.

"That's hard to explain in words, but the taste always tells the truth," Opa said with a twinkle in his eyes.

He looked at the can now in his hand, satisfied, and drank its entire contents in one wistful gulp. He considered leaping into the water, just like he had as a boy, while Opa watched. He put the thought aside, remembering he didn't have a swimsuit with him. The rays of the sun danced across the water, twinkling brighter than the stars would in the sky. With the sapphire waters and the light breezes that rustled through the emerald trees, he felt as if this were his own little world, a world where only magic and bliss existed.

That summer he had stayed longer at his grandparent's house than usual, which was odd since school was starting in less than a week. One night the humidity kept him up most of the night. Just as he was about to take sleep's hand, his grandmother's voice nudged him awake.

"How much time does he have left?" Oma asked.

The words were at first alien and incomprehensible. Then he heard his grandmother's broken voice say to the person at the other end of phone, "Oh, okay… that's not much… No, my apologies… It's not your fault. Opa's… pancreatic. You've done all you could… Yes, we… We'll be there for another appointment… On Saturday…"

He had tried to stay hidden, but Oma had spotted him as soon as she turned in his direction.

"Earl, what are you doing? You're supposed to be in bed."

"What's wrong with Opa?"

"Nothing," Oma insisted with tears in her eyes.

Earl was confused and tried to reach some kind of understanding. Pan-cre-a-tic. A strange word. What was that? He turned it over in his mind.

"Is Opa taking me to see Peter Pan?" Earl asked.

Oma, tears welling in her eyes, tried to force a smile. "No. But he still wants to take you somewhere. To give you something."

"What?"

Oma started, "Mem…"

Earl stared at the water from his perch on the pier. His fishing trip had been a success. He wondered if it would have been more bountiful with a boat. He recalled his grandfather's boat, *Lillian*. The funeral had followed some time later, and there was no coffin, only his boat. As *Lillian* was lowered into the ground, Earl couldn't help but think how strange it was to have been buried in a boat. In a way, it made sense.

Sitting there, he turned the familiar deck of playing cards in his hands, and was reminded of his favourite child game. He gazed back to the old red pick-up truck and its weathered licensed plate: G0 F1SH. He set the cards down and picked up his fishing rod. As he settled in, a passing jogger stopped and nodded at him.

"Fishing?" he asked.

"Yep," Earl said, pulling an empty line from the water.

The runner snickered. "You're not going to catch anything like that. What are you hoping to catch?"

"Memories."

RUNNER UP

The World Was Quiet

Charlotte Strathy

Throughout my life, I was quiet, and the world around me was too. It was either pure, unadulterated silence, or deafening sounds, like nails on a chalkboard. I could never appreciate the world's ambience around me. Music tore my eardrums, whether it be classic Mozart or blaring pop songs. Voices as soft as whispers came out as shrieks and wails through a broken microphone.

The silence was the worst. In my lonely, somber thoughts, the world around me would go quiet. It did that a lot, and I hated it. I wanted to appreciate the passion artists put in their lyrics, the laughter of happy people receiving good news, the noise a gentle breeze makes when it carries the chirping of birds. All those wonderful noises, but it all came out as garbled, loud nonsense in my ears.

Until I met her.

She moved here over the March break. I noticed her the moment I walked into English class, sitting in the empty desk next to mine. Her hair was an inky abyss tied back with a sunset orange scrunchie. Her skin was dark, her eyes not much darker. The way she sweetly smiled at me as I sat down was oddly charming. A social butterfly I presumed, and a visually captivating one as well. I paid no mind to her, despite wanting nothing more than to look at her. The teacher, in his static filled voice, addressed her as Marion. In that same voice he asked her to tell the class about herself.

When she spoke, I sat up straight and looked her way. My ears couldn't possibly have deceived me. They'd never heard something so wonderful before. Her voice was soft like the fluffy feathers on baby penguins, sweet like fresh honey. It was as though she belonged in a heavenly choir. I was determined to become her friend at that moment.

She was easy to talk to and patient with my quiet voice and shy tendencies. The thing is, I didn't want to talk to her. I wanted her to talk to me. I wanted nothing more than to hear her voice, but something about her made me begin to speak up. I'd never liked my voice. It's too deep for someone like me. But the way she perked up when I spoke, I noticed my voice had a certain, silk smooth charm to it once I started talking about the things I liked.

As I hung out with her over the course of the semester, more extraordinary things began happening. My teachers, their voices like broken radios, started sounding like they'd been tuned to the right frequency. The music, the music Marion liked, sounded less like tearing horror and more like the beautiful symphonies they were meant to be. People talked to me with real voices, and I began to talk back to them. Even when I was alone, there was never the sound of lonely silence in my head. Marion had brought music to my ears, whether she realised it or not. She was new, so she couldn't tell. My peers noticed and started trying to become friends with me. This new found music to my ears improved my attitude and performance, and my teachers were happily surprised when they gave me A's and B's.

People looked at how much Marion and I hung out and thought nothing of it. If anything, we were "Just gals being pals!" I, however, knew that wasn't the case for me. This wasn't simply friendship, not even best-friendship. It didn't feel like either of those. I looked at Marion and felt like I was going to light on fire. I heard her speak and could barely hear her over my pounding heartbeat. This wasn't friendship, this was love, and I loved Marion.

It was the last day of school when I finally told her. She greeted me as usual, with her lovely voice. I greeted her back. My face was on fire, my chest about to burst. I took in a deep breath and, with my voice that's slightly too deep for a girl, I told her. I told her about how she was the first pleasant noise I'd heard, about the music she'd brought to my ears, the way the world was no longer just deafening noise. But before she could tell me anything, her dad had honked the car horn. It was the first horrid noise I had heard in a long time, but she sweetly said goodbye and that was all.

June ended without her saying a word. July was the month it happened.

I'd never been one for coffee shops, but I decided to go down anyway, to see if they at least had good pastries. I entered, listening to the little chime of the bell above the door. My eyes gazed over the muffins, the croissants, and the scones. Then they landed on her, and a boy. Marion introduced him in her sweet voice, but I didn't catch his name. Then she explained how it was their one month anniversary. It hadn't occurred to me until later that it was also exactly one month since I'd confessed to her. However, I didn't need to know that for it to be any more painful. My face started to burn up, my eyes blurring with tears. I asked her why. Why she didn't return my feelings. Why she ignored me for so long. Why she couldn't have said no in the first place.

She tried to talk to me, but then her sweet voice began to change. It began crackling, then it sounded like she was screaming at me. The noises of the coffee shop around me grew louder and louder, tearing through my ears and digging into my brain as tears rolled down my burning cheeks. The clatter of teacups ground against my eardrums. The chatter around us, about us, it was driving me insane. I didn't hear her explanation, but it's not like it would've made a difference. Marion left the shop with her boyfriend, and I was alone. I'd never felt so alone, so sombre, so horrendous. My thoughts were cursing me, patronising my misery.

Then the world went silent. Not a sound. It hadn't happened in a long time, my thoughts muting the world. And I knew that it was not only the last time it would happen, but that now it wouldn't stop. The only thing that could bring me back would be Marion, but she'd never talk to me again. Standing in the middle of a crowded coffee shop, patrons and servers staring at me without so much as a peep, I came to a realisation. Without Marion, I was quiet.

Without her, the world was quiet.

RUNNER UP

Tip Toe

Zowie Decunha

Wake Up.

Get out of bed.

Get dressed.

Breakfast.

Walk to school.

Days go by and the same routine follows. The same things happen. No ripples in the tide that is my life. At least that's how it used to be before everything changed.

When I walked to school, I would constantly stroll past one specific building. It had one window that always stuck out to me. It was always an exciting ripple effect as I stood there watching. Beautiful music could be heard from inside when the door was left open. The cool air would flow into the building and hot air out.

I would stand outside the window, watching the beautiful people carefully walk, step by step, gracefully to their final destination, then they would swirl and bow. All with slow, steady and beautiful movements. Their hair was always done up in a tight bun, neatly sitting on the tops of their heads. They all wore black tight shirts and pants, with no shoes.

Could they be any more graceful?

"Sabrina! We have to go. We'll be late!" My Mother quickly grabbed my hand and pulled me away, leaving the beautiful and graceful pieces of art behind me as we enter the school.

* * * * *

"Okay, so, Sabrina, how is your day going?" The familiar question rang in my ears, and the usual voice had found its way into my head, within the same-old dimly lit classroom.

"Hi, Mr. Darwin, could you watch Sabrina after school today? I have to tutor a Grade 11 in the English department." My Mother had asked the other teachers in my department, but couldn't find anyone, and I knew Mr. Darwin was her last hope.

"Of course I can. We'll have a good day." Mr. Darwin gave my mother a soft smile.

"Oh, my gosh, thank you! You're a lifesaver! Now remember to follow this schedule. At 9:30 p.m. is her T.V. time, and at 10:00 p.m. she enjoys..." My mother continued telling Mr. Darwin the schedule as I stared absently at a colourful poster. It highlighted the words "Bully Free Environment" in different colours. It had blocks of purple and circles of orange, almost as significant as the graceful movement of the people down the street.

"Wow, your mother has a very concentrated schedule for you, doesn't she?" I hummed in response, proving I acknowledged what he said, but never taking my eyes off the poster that was in front of me.

"Well, does your mother ever ask you what you want to do?" The question caught me off guard, and I looked over to the man who I thought was like the rest, someone who would follow the schedule that was laid out for me ever so perfectly.

"Your Mother did explain that the only unusual thing in your schedule is that you stop at the dance studio every day. Every day. She told me not to take you there, and that it's only a phase, but she did put me in charge of you today so..." He looked at me with a small grin as if reading my mind.

I did want to go there. I did want to watch the slow movements of the unknown people who danced beyond the small glass window.

"Would you like to go?"

I studied him for a couple of minutes, before slowly nodding my head.

"Don't worry about getting in. My wife Melinda is an instructor there." He took my arm and led me out of the classroom.

That's when I noticed the eyes. There were around 1500 students in this high school, and I could feel at least half of their eyes on me as we walked through the cafeteria. The eyes were burning through my back as we walked. We passed a group of students, and it was almost as if the whole world had slowed down. The group of students were staring at me, not even blinking, watching as Mr. Darwin and I walked out the front doors.

My breathing had picked up and my blood was rushing. I was starting to get dizzy and my legs were becoming weak.

"Sabrina, concentrate." The voice was so quiet compared to the pounding of my racing heart. "Sabrina, its okay. Sabrina?" I couldn't concentrate. Everything was starting to become dark. "Sabrina look at me, look at me." I did as he said. My hands were fidgeting with my shirt. I knew I might faint or pass out from hyperventilation. "Look we made it." He smiled at me and smiled, That's when I realised we had walked the whole entire way to the small building with a single window... the flow of hot air slowly coming from the door.

I gasped, surprised by the random change I didn't understand. It was amazing.

"Let's go in, shall we?" He lightly pulled me into the small building where a slow stream of music was coming from the front on an iPod shuffle.

"I love this song. It's adorable," Mr. Darwin announced absently. I looked at the iPod, and saw the song Apologise by Matilda (feat. OMVR). It was beautiful, just like the people moving to it.

"Hi, Hon. What are you doing here?" A smaller women came over to Mr. Darwin and lightly kissed him on the cheek.

"Well, I'm here with Sabrina, and I think Sabrina would like to dance." I look over to Mr. Darwin. Why would I dance? I can barely stay on my feet as it is.

"Well then, Sabrina, why don't you come with me." She took my hand and led me to another room. It was brightly lit, which irritated my eyes, and there were mirrors all around me. All I could see was my reflection, my blue eyes and blonde hair, my skinny frame. I could see... me. My mother never let me look at myself.

"Well, let's see what you've got then." Melinda smiled and turned on the song that had been playing in the hallway. "Remember don't be afraid. It's okay if you can't actually dance. We can teach you. But we have to know what you can do first."

Slowly the song started to play, filling the studio until it was all I could hear. The slow rhythm had taken over my body, and somehow naturally I started to sway to the beat. I didn't even know what was happening anymore. I was so distracted by the music, I didn't remember anything. I couldn't remember anything: the schedule, the anxiety, the staring eyes. All was so easily gone and out of my mind as I followed what the other people had done earlier and I moved just like them, never quite reaching my limits.

When the song was over, I was panting. My breathing had picked up and my heart was racing, but not from the anxiety that once ruled my body. A new feeling... I had never felt before. I stared at myself wide eyed. I did that. A small grin slipped onto my face. I did that?!

"You have natural talent don't you? You could go places.

How did you actually do that?!" Melinda's face was bright with excitement.

"Y-Y-" That's when I noticed my mother standing in the doorway to the small room. She must have seen me, because she was in tears. I had never seen my Mom so sad. But then again, maybe it was happiness on her face. I was sure she had never seen me so happy.

*****

Several years later, here I am, competing in a national competition.

Mr. Darwin and his wife stayed with me through the whole journey. They helped me get to where I am now. My mother had seen how happy I was, and she agreed to allow me to follow the road that had been placed so clearly in front of me.

Since that first small dance, I have come so far. My whole life has changed, and I love how it's changed. Now I know I can do anything, become anything, and achieve anything. I don't fear those staring eyes any longer.

Mr. Darwin showed me a quote that inspired me to go further, and it got me here, on this stage, holding the first place trophy!

"Everybody is a genius. But if you judge a fish on its ability to climb a tree, it will live its whole life believing it was stupid." – Albert Einstein.

I was like the fish. I had felt so stupid, until I achieved what I had thought was impossible.

RUNNER UP

The Boy in the Bright Pink Hoodie

Angela Tozer

I don't remember clearly the first time I saw him, unlike most love stories. Most people have a definite first memory of seeing the person they love, but he had always just been there in the periphery. When he was younger, he was soft and nerdy. Slightly chubby, he was childishly cute and kinder than anyone.

By Grade 8, he was still soft-ish, with glasses and very short hair. His first announcement that year was that he was going off on a trip with his family. They would be going to Los Angeles first, and then to Kenya. He was gone for most of the year, leaving late September and returning late May. He came back... different. His once shaved hair was now long enough that it fluffed over his ears, and it was now obvious that his hair was curly and almost black. The top was distinctly longer than the sides, but not by much. He was a few inches taller now, meaning he wasn't as obnoxiously short. His smile was wider, happier, and that happiness was infectious.

I guess the first time I really saw him, though, was January of grade nine. We had just got back from Christmas vacation. I was wearing a pleated yellow skirt, one of my favourites, with a white short sleeved shirt tucked into it. I went about my day pretty normally. When I entered the caf for lunch, something was different. I looked around. He was sitting with the jocks today, and over the back of his chair, a varsity jacket.

He made varsity football in grade nine. What truly shocked me, though, was that he wasn't wearing it. He was instead wearing a hot pink hoodie with his soccer number on the back.

He was surrounded by varsity boys and looked like he was a little uncomfortable, but they were joking and shoving each other. He was smiling now. It truly transformed him. I smiled quietly to myself.

A few weeks later, I watched him play football. He was magnificent at it. As a running back, he was speedy strong. It was hard to watch him get tackle when he did, but even though he was smaller than most of the other players, he was usually fast enough to startle them or strong enough to knock them over.

I probably realized that I like-liked him in late March. We were at a party, and of course, the host brought out a glass bottle. It was Spin The Bottle time, and I hadn't yet had my first kiss. I sat in the circle at first, but about ten seconds in, I backed out. I didn't want him to see me kiss someone else. I wanted to kiss him, but the chance that I would have to kiss someone else was too much for me.

By Grade 10 he had changed even more. He had muscled up and cut his hair over the summer. The loss of his hair was a little sad, but I still liked him. Some girls fall out of love after the loss of the hair, but not me. I fall in love with personality, not looks, and his smile and kindness were still the same. I didn't talk to him often, but when I did, I was always struck by his kindness.

But other girls were beginning to catch his eye. Girls that weren't me. I didn't mind. I wasn't exceptionally good looking. I was short-haired, and not particularly curvy. I wasn't overly flat-chested, but I was boyish, and often tried to hide my chest. I was sure that he saw me more as "one of the boys" than part of his dating pool. I was surprisingly okay with that though. As long as he was happy and I could keep watching him smile, I would deal with the shot to the heart every day watching him with his girlfriend.

A week later, it finally happened. He got a girlfriend who wasn't me. He was happy.

And so was I.

GRADES 7 - 8

1st PLACE

Circle

McKenna McFatridge

And spin, and spin, and spin…

You don't truly know love until you know the softly emitted sound of a record player as the needle slowly winds its way to the first track.

That's something my grandfather used to say to me. He always thought that the soft buzzing noise, surrounding you and filling the room with white noise, made you know that you were, indeed, truly human. I couldn't agree more.

He was part of a "Monthly Record Club". The first Tuesday of every month the mailman would come to the door bearing a sizeable, flat rectangular box with "do not bend" hastily scrawled across it. When my mom was little she said that he used to refer to it as "a magic disc" – which for him, it truly was.

It magically turned a hobby into an obsession.

There used to be a game my cousins and I would play – I don't remember the exact name of it now, something along the lines of "Grandpa's Labyrinth" – where we would try to navigate his maze. The records were stacked into huge barricades everywhere, you'd scramble over a pile here, and leap across one there in an attempt to get to the one that you knew had your favourite album in it. If you got to it first, you were the winner, and it was your music choice that day.

I won a lot.

Mom always said that I was grandpa's favourite anyway, and that she thought he rigged it so that I would always win.

She was always bitter when she said it, like her super-glued smile wasn't quite dry and slowly dipped down to become lopsided. At the time, I never got it, why she was always so upset when it came to her dad, but I think I understand now.

While those records created my childhood, sitting on the chesterfield and watching black circles spin round and round, they mouldered my mother's. He was so obsessed with them, as collecting more and more would fill some void inside of him. He completely renovated the house because he needed more room to store them. There was a constant influx of them, and like a black hole, he was just sucked in more and more.

When he went, and we had to clean up his house, I picked out my favourites in a pattern that by that point was well memorised. Up, down, over -- *Folsom Prison Blues*. Left, right, jump -- *The Dark Side of the Moon*. Down, down, up – *Monsters*. Over, left, down – *Abbey Road*.

By the end I had around twenty vinyls in my arms (a miracle that I could hold them all) and dropped them off in the car. I also snagged the record player he always kept on the coffee table; it was well-loved, and he took care of it as if it were his child. While mom was busy figuring out what to do with the furniture, I had already driven off to drop the records and player off in my room at home before she noticed I'd taken them.

I still have his whole life's collection. I went back every day, stuffing them in my closet, under the bed, between books on the bookshelf. At the time I thought I was being clever and sneaky, but I'm fairly certain that my mother eventually noticed – but if she cared, she didn't say anything. I think she was happy he wasn't her problem anymore.

I have my own apartment now and storage solutions that don't include building myself a maze, and I can listen to my records freely again. I don't think it was ever that I couldn't listen to the vinyls, I just tried to avoid them – I think they'd hurt my mom. I like listening to the ones he used to play the most, the ones that we'd listen to together while he'd tell me about his memories growing up, when he first heard them, and the stories behind them.

He used to tell me that life was all but a record playing – you spin around and around waiting to start and end, stumbling over some bits and sometimes other bits are scratched. If he were to hear himself now, I think he'd say that his life right now was scratched, jumping over bits that not even taping a dime onto the needle can fix.

He liked to say that with a record you can always flip to Side B if you didn't like A, but I think he's forgotten everything on A, and is stuck slowly spinning to the centre of B.

But those records, they made him so happy – they made me so happy – he spun me memories, and I feel like I have to return the favour, you know?"

"I know –" He paused for a moment, rough, calloused hands resting on my knee for a second. He eyed my name tag and stumbles out, "Stephie."

He eyes dimmed for a moment. I could see his mind spinning like his beloved records before he softly said, "I think I know someone named Stephie."

"I'm sure you did. Maybe you've just forgotten."

He chuckled, and I gave him his pick and set it up, just like he did for me so many years ago.

And as I left, the record player started to spin, and spin, and spin...

2nd PLACE

The Man With the Yellow Scarf

Annika Lusis

Thomas wasn't used to getting lost. This was his first time. One minute his mom was standing beside him at the Sunday Farmer's market, the next she was gone. He searched for an exit in the hopes she would be outside. When he found it his little arms swung the door open just enough so he could fit through. He gazed around but his mother was nowhere to be found. He began to whimper as all five year olds do who have lost their mothers. Salty tears sprang out his big eyes. He wiped them away with his hands. Hearing footsteps he looked in the hopes it was his mother but instead it was the silent old man with the yellow scarf. He thought the old man would just walk by him like he always did, but to his surprise the man stopped when he saw Thomas.

"Everything alright down there?" the old man asked him. "You look like you're in a bit of distress lad."

Thomas's parents had never given him the talk about not speaking to strangers, so he answered the man truthfully, "I can't find my mummy."

"Oh dear, do you know your mummy's name?" the man asked him.

Thomas thought for a second. He had never taken the time to ask his mother what her actual name was other than "mum".

"No." Thomas shrugged.

"Alrighty, what's your name lad?" the man sighed, his Sunday clearly not what he had imagined it would be.

"Thomas Eden Divers," he said proudly. Thomas liked his name; his mom always said Thomas was a strong name.

"Well, Divers, happy to make your acquaintance," the man said shaking the small boy's hand with a much stronger grip than intended.

Wincing under the clasp of the man's grip, Thomas shook back hastily.

"So Divers, err, where do you live?" he asked.

Thomas pondered once again. All he could remember was that he lived in a red brick house on a corner.

"I don't know," he said.

"Do you live in town?"

He was proud to know the answer to this question. "Yes."

The man thought for a second.

"Do you live nearby?" he asked him.

"I think so." Thomas nodded.

"Do your parents work around here?" he asked, running out of ideas.

"Mummy works in that clothes store. I have to go there all the time." Thomas groaned recalling all of the days spent in that little boring shop.

"What about your dad?"

"I don't have a dad," replied Thomas. This was true; mum had never told him anything about a dad. "I've always wanted one though," Thomas admitted.

"Ok, Divers, first we're going to find your mother's work, then where you live and get you home," smiled the old man, his scarf blowing in the wind like a superhero.

"Let's go," Thomas bellowed, running down the street towards the shop.

Behind him the old man was having trouble keeping up. "Divers, wait up," he cried.

Thomas waited for him at the door of the dark and empty shop.

"Drat, closed," cursed the man, out of breath. "What other shops does your mom like to go to?"

Thomas pointed a small finger across the road at a bakery. "She always gets me chocolate chip cookies there when I'm good," he explained.

"Okay, will someone recognise you there?" the man asked, still out of breath.

"The lady behind the machine will," he assured him. "She says I'm her favourite customer!"

"I bet you are." smiled the old man. "Okay, come on, let's cross the street." He grabbed Thomas's hand and walked him across the street. They walked into the small crowded bakery. Thomas followed the old man to the cashier, still gripping his warm hand. "Hi, can I help you?" asked the woman behind the machine.

"I'm okay, thank you. I was wondering if you could help me get Thomas here home?" asked the man.

"Oh, it's little Thomas. Hi!" She grinned.

"Hi." Thomas grinned back.

"We do have Thomas' address in our book somewhere for regular deliveries. I'll give it to you when I have a minute, as we're very busy now. Can you wait for five minutes or so?" she asked.

"That will work," smiled the man. "We'll go to the park to kill some time. Be back in ten minutes"

"Sure," said the woman. "I'll have it ready by then."

Thomas and the old man walked down to the nearby playground and waited. Growing anxious Thomas turned to the man. "How come you always wear that scarf?" he asked curiously.

"My wife knitted it for me years ago. I never wore it because I thought it was too bright, but now that she's gone, I realised my life could use a little brightening up," the man explained sadly.

"Oh," said Thomas, beginning to feel sad himself. "Sorry."
"No need to apologise. She had a great life." The man smiled. "Everyone's gotta go at some point."

Now Thomas started to cry.

"Don't cry, Divers." said the man patting him on his shoulder.

"I miss mom so much," sniffled Thomas. "What if I never see her again?"

"You will see her again, I promise," said the man.

"Pinky promise?"

"Pinky promise?" the man asked, confused. "What's that?"

"It's a promise that can never be broken, and it's made by a pinky," Thomas explained. "Like this." He stuck out his pinky to the man. "Now you stick out yours," Thomas said to him.

The old man did.

"Now they lock onto each other." He smiled. "And shake."

They did and let go. Thomas wiped his running nose.

"Brighten up, Divers It's almost time to head back to the cafe." He smiled, handing Thomas a handkerchief. "In the meantime, how about we play some pirates or something?"

Thomas grinned. "I call being captain!" he squealed.

"Aye aye, Captain Divers"

The man grabbed a stick and handed it to Thomas. "Your sword, Captain Divers.´´ He bowed, raising his own. "A duel?"

"It's on," sneered Thomas.

After few minutes of stabbing one other Thomas was tired. The man lifted the five year old into his arms and carried him back to the cafe.

"The address is 21 Clamber Street. It's around the block," said the woman when they got back.

"Thank you so much for your help." The man beamed at her then Thomas.

Feeling a little better Thomas beamed back.

"Actually, by any chance Thomas are you hungry?" asked the man.

"Yes," considered Thomas. "Starving."

"Shall we get a snack for the road then?" the man grinned at him. "How about those chocolate cookies you were going on about?"

"Yes please!" Thomas squealed.

The woman came back with a cookie placed on a small china plate.

"There you go dearie," she said, smiling widely, dimples beginning to appear.

Thomas quickly snatched the cookie, stuffing his face with the chocolate goodness.

"Thank you," he said through a mouthful.

"You're welcome dear. Now run along to your mother. She must be worried sick," said the woman.

Thomas knew this was true, so he and the old man ran out the door. This time the man was able to keep up. Finally, they arrived at the small red brick house on the corner.

"Well then, Divers, it has come to the time where we have to part," sighed the man.

"What does that mean?"

"Well it's another way to say it's time for goodbye," he explained.

"No, I don't want you to go!" cried Thomas, hanging onto the man's leg. "I had so much fun with you. What if I don't see you again? What if I forget you?"

The old man crouched down, took off his bright scarf and wrapped it around Thomas. "Here, Divers. Now you will never forget me, because now you have a part of me," he said softly.

"But this is all you have left of your love," said Thomas.

"No, not really. She's everywhere." The man smiled. "The people you love never really leave you for good."

Thomas didn't fully understand this, but he played along anyway. He was having a moment. "Will I ever see you again?" he asked hopefully.

The man hesitated. "Maybe one day fate will cross our paths again."

"I really hope so," Thomas said, giving the man one last hug.

"Now go and explain to your mother where you've been." advised the man.

So Thomas ran to his doorstep, but not before smiling at the kind old man one more time, hugging his new scarf. And even though his mother screeched at him for an hour straight about leaving her side, he kept grinning to himself.

Thomas never saw the man ever again after that day, but he would go on for the rest of his life wearing the bright yellow scarf.

3rd PLACE

The Girl Who Loved the Sky

Alex Petrie

What would you do if the world turned grey and peoples' faces became square and electronic? I turned to the sky. Its stunning blue was still unmarred by the filth of the humans below. Its soft white clouds were pristine, untouched by those who would ruin them. So I watched, forgetting about the grey grass and steel trees around me. I forgot the roar of the metal machines, the din of the city and the chatter of the electronic people. I watched the beautiful sky, and the sky watched back. The smoke and smog in the streets below clogged the lungs of all passers-by. The chemical world that we'd built slowly suffocated us all. None of this mattered when I looked at the sky and the clouds sluggishly floating by. I lay there, among the artificial grass and trees. I could have stayed there for all eternity, but the day turned to night. The stars shone dimly in the sky, as if their light was going out. I went to sleep inside, under my roof of steel and stone, unable to see the stars.

As sleep took me I heard whispering in the shadows of my mind. I found myself in the night sky, soaring above the clouds and among the stars. I looked at my bare feet and saw rock beneath my toes. No soil or earth, just hard rock. I turned to see a kind-looking elderly man sitting on the stone. His leathery skin was wrinkled around his eyes, showing smile lines, but he wasn't smiling then. He looked sad and lonely, like life had drained the joy out of him. He looked at me, his eyes piercing and intelligent. When he spoke his voice was low and raspy, as if he hadn't spoken in a thousand years.

"Dear child, tell me, why dream of the cold, lonesome faraway sky?" His calm simple words seem to cut into my heart, stripping away my walls and barriers. He revealed the small girl who loved the sky and how scared of the world she really was. I didn't understand how such simple words could affect me so, but they brought out my anger and fear of the world. A small tear fell down my cheek as I considered my answer, scared to speak.

"Tell me, dear child, why do you cry?" I tried to swallow my tears, to no avail for they clogged my throat. His words sat still in the silent air, interrupted only by my soft sobbing. I tried again to regain my composure, but again failed. His question burned in my head, and before I could think I was spewing out an answer.

"There's nothing down there on the ground! The machines drown out the laughter and are ever so loud! The trees are plastic and nothing is green! It's all grey and muted, never once do I hear joy resonating around me! Nothing but emotionless electronic din and false laughter!" I cried out, the ugly words falling quickly and angrily from my lips. The man's expression hadn't changed from quiet calm. This frustrated me. I was so tired of people being mechanically calm all the time. I wanted them to scream and shout. I wanted them to cry or laugh. Anything! I wanted my mother to scold me when I did something wrong or to laugh and smile when I did well. I wanted my friends to run and laugh out in the schoolyard instead of staying inside on screens. I was so tired of people living in the screens, forgetting about the outside world. I wanted them to be alive and joyful. I wanted them to be human!!

This man, I thought, would understand! I thought he who was alone might know my pain, though I don't know why. He sat and did nothing on his rock, remaining as emotionless as the rest of them. I kicked at the rock with my bare feet, bloodying my toes. The pain felt good, and hot tears rolled down my icy cheeks.

"Child do not mistake me for a machine," the man interrupted. I looked into his eyes to find his calm had slipped away. His eyes were sad and old as if they had seen too much pain, but another emotion lurked under his sadness; anger.

"I have seen and done much, I'm not glued to a screen. My home was once like yours, happy and free. Then it all slipped away, the laughter and joy, replaced by the machine calm and the artificial. My world shrivelled and withered, until it was but a stone, hardened and lonely. I watched this and could not stop it, so I now sit and regret. I now watch the cold stars fly by. I am alone, the last of my people, a foolish old man. I now urge you to return home. Look not to the sky for help, but to your people, the ones who still smile. Find them and work to find others. Plant trees and flowers, remind the world of who they are. They are not slaves to machines, they are human beings that have free will and can make their own choices. Find them and teach them to laugh and cry. To become angry, to remain calm, but above all else, to love. Remind the world of how to love."

He finished with tears in his soft eyes. He took my hand in his own, his calloused skin warm and rough against my own. He pressed a small object into my hand and closed my fingers around it.

"Fly home child. Save your home. You can always go on as long as you have hope." He brushed the tears from my eyes, and his mouth split into a smile.

"Plant it for me," he whispered. He then dissolved into light, fracturing apart and flying away. He flew into the cold sky and left behind him a feeling of warmth and happiness. He became a bright star in the cold night, and I followed the star home. I awoke in my bed with a lighter heart then when I fell asleep. In my hand I still clutched the object he had given me, it was a tiny seed.

A seed of hope.

I took some earth, placed it in a cup on my window sill and planted the seed. I then rushed off to school, close to being late. It was during the break that I saw her, a small girl, about my age. Alone in the cold outside, shivering in the corner of the cramped concrete playground, her dark skin contrasted against the grey of the courtyard. She was crying. Not a fake cry, nor were her eyes simply watering, but truly crying, letting her fear, anger, and sadness out into the world. I walked up to her and held her to my chest, stroking her hair while she cried into my shoulder. Afterwards, we spoke about school and family, about the loss of her grandmother, and of her grandmother's life and her legacy. She spoke of her stories, and laughed. Like me, she was someone who still felt the world. It was there in the schoolyard that we became friends and I told her of my dream. She didn't laugh or make fun of me, but simply asked to see the seed. When I returned home she came with me. I almost ran to my window and looked at the cup where I had buried the seed. A flower had bloomed, a small white blossom that smelled of sunshine and fresh air. Hope bloomed in my heart and in the cup.

The girl and I made a pact to save our world and its people. We found those who still laughed and cried, and we showed them our flower of hope. We spoke to others and explained how grey their world was and showed them the flower. Some only laughed and walked away, but others listened and stayed. Whispers spread about our flower of hope, and the people who listened told others, and one day, we saw a second flower had sprouted in a park. People now laughed more and cried more. We replanted the trees and grass until the world was once again green. We taught people to love, and more flowers grew until the world was once again full of joy and completely free.

I will still look at the girl by my side and smile, before turning back to watch the bright stars in the sky, watching the star that was the old man glow brightly with happiness, because I had planted his seed of hope.

RUNNER UP

Wings of the Storm

Callista Pitman

I stand. Waiting. Breathing. In, out. In, out. Anything to calm my nerves.

One of the assistants brings me the uniform. I pull on the boots, fingerless gloves, and goggles.

Then I pick up my wings.

It's my first time holding them, as apprentices are not allowed to touch them. Mine are grey, as I've seen from afar all these years. But up close, they are many shades, glittering like rain. I wonder why this colour was chosen for me.

I strap them on, buckling them to my shoulders, wrists, elbows, and torso. The leather straps are soft against my arms, and they don't restrict my arm's movement.

This will be my first flight. We have to apprentice for many years to become a flier. I can't remember ever seeing anybody other then the other apprentices and our masters, though I'm told that I was born outside of our grounds.

The fliers' missions are, as always, to guide stormclouds to where rain is needed. And to stay hidden from other humans.

I walk forwards, to the edge of the roof. The wind tugs gently at my wings, and I look up at the sky. A stormcloud hovers above me. Footsteps sound behind me, and I turn to see my master approaching.

"Your time has come. Remember, only let it rain where it is needed, and do not let anyone see you. Your entire existence revolves around the moment you give rain." His white hair blows in the wind.

I nod, straightening up and taking a deep breath.

"Go, now." He nods back to me.

I step forward, my boots clacking on the shingles. Wind whips at my long hair. I shake it away as I stand on the tip of the roof, eyes trained on the cloud above me. My heart beats fast in my chest, a steady thrumming that somehow calms me.

Bending my knees, I spread my arms as I've been taught. The wind catches my wings, and in one fluid motion I spring from the roof, pushing off my toes. The wind tosses me around for a moment, and I angle my arms so I'm supported by the wind currents.

Steadier now, I rise until I'm covered with the grey mist of the stormcloud. It shimmers with a thousand colours, brushing against my skin like feathers. I drop my arms lower, letting my wings catch a weaker air current. Once I've drifted behind the cloud, I shift again to a stronger current that whips my hair, pushing me along with the cloud.

Spreading my arms wide, I guide the stormcloud as I've been trained, scanning the land below for somewhere that needs rain.

I glide above forests that look like a smudge of green paint, meadows of colourful flowers dancing in the wind and patchworks of farming fields that look like a autumn coloured quilt. The colours are more intense and beautiful then anything I've ever seen before.

My wings are built powerfully, like an eagle or a hawk, and it takes hardly any effort to stay airborne.

Finally I pass over a parched field. I stop my stormcloud and hover. The ground is cracked and dry, like your lips when your desperately thirsty. There's little grass, and the patches that are left are brittle and dry.

Perfect.

I immerse myself in the stormcloud once again, this time spinning in circles, stirring up the grey fog. The cloud is heavy with rain, and it doesn't take much urging for it to start pouring on the land below. The freedom and power fills my chest and makes me feel lighter then the cloud. The field below slowly deepens from dusty beige to rich brown, and the grass perks up and begins to green.

The raindrops shimmer as they fall, making a steady drumming sound on the earth below.

Lightning flashes, brightening the world around it, and a few seconds later, thunder cracks loudly. I can feel the vibration of the sound in my chest as I hover next to the cloud. I don't know how long I hover, transfixed by the storm, but finally my cloud stops raining, and drifts away, white and light as a feather.

I shake my head, pulling myself from my trance as I turn to glide home.

This time I soar quicker, catching a strong air current.

The landscape flashes by in a multicoloured blur below me, and my eyes dart back and forth, trying to take in the vast beauty of the outside world, a world I'd seen little of before today. All too soon I spot the roof I took off from.

Not ready to land quite yet, I circle the building, closing my eyes to memorize the feeling of wind in my hair.

I take a breath and lower until I can see every shingle on the roof. My toes touch the shingles, and I land lightly on the roof, letting my arms fall to my sides. My master is waiting.

"How was it?" he asks with a smile.

I push my goggles up and shake my tangled hair out of my face. I turn, gazing at the sky, reflecting on my flight.

Then I quickly spin to face him, grinning. "When can I go again?"

RUNNER UP

How the Pelican Got His Beak

Graeme Bissell

Hello! I was expecting you. I believe you've come to hear about how the pelican got his beak, yes? Ah, well you have come to the right place. Today the pelican has quite a curious beak, but it wasn't always like that… Long, long ago the pelican looked much like every other bird but with a long, long spear-like beak. He used his long, long spear-like beak to catch fish, and he was an amazing fisherman. In fact, he could fish in any imaginable direction! But there is one other thing you should know about Pelican. He was very, very proud of his long, long spear-like beak and his amazing fishing skills. Other animals such as Dolphin, Seagull and Man could not catch enough fish to feed their families because Pelican was taking all the fish.

One day, Man, Dolphin, and Seagull all decided they must teach Pelican to be humbler, so they formulated a plan. A little while later, Man approached Pelican while he was fishing. "Hey Pelican! How much water do you think you can fit in that beak you're so proud of?" asked Man.

Pelican replied, "I bet I could fit more water in my beak than you ever could fit in your pitiful mouth."

Man angrily retorted, "Oh yeah! Prove it."

So Pelican started filling and filling his beak with water until he could fit no more. After Pelican had finished filling his beak with water, Man told Pelican, "Really? That's all the water you can fit in that beak you're so proud of? I'm sorely disappointed in you, Pelican."

Then Pelican let all the water out of his beak, and the man noticed that Pelican's long, long spear-like beak was a little less than spear-like, and it had started to sag.

Later that day, Dolphin came across Pelican while he was fishing and asked, "Hey Pelican! How much water do you think can fit in that beak you're so proud of?"

Pelican answered, "I can fit more water in this wonderful beak of mine than you could ever fit in that pitiful mouth of yours."

Dolphin replied, "Prove it."

So once again, Pelican filled and filled and filled his beak until he could fit no more water inside his long, but not so spear-like beak. Pelican didn't notice that he could fit more water than before. Dolphin pretended to be disappointed and said, "Oh, I thought you could fit more water in that beak you're so proud of."

After Dolphin finished talking, Pelican let the water out of his beak, and Dolphin was pleased to see that Pelican's not so spear-like beak was now bulkier and even less spear-like.

Later in the evening of that very same day, Seagull came across Pelican while he was fishing. Before Seagull could say anything, Pelican said, "Let me guess, you want to know how much water will fit in my magnificent beak."

Seagull, surprised by Pelican's anticipation of his request, said kindly, "Yes, I do want to know how much water will fit in your magnificent beak. Would you please show me?"

"I suspect something is going on because both Man and Dolphin have challenged me in the same way," thought Pelican, but for the third time that day, he filled and filled and filled his bulky beak that now sagged very much. When he could fit no more water in it, he stopped. Once again Pelican did not notice that he could fit more water than ever before in his new curious-looking beak.

Seagull said, "WOW! That is a lot of water you can fit in your beak."

Pelican replied, "You really think so?"

"Yes, definitely. But you look different from when I last saw you. Here, take a look in this mirror," Seagull said.

Pelican looked in the mirror and what he saw astonished him. He no longer saw a striking thin beak. Instead, he saw a bulky one. It took time for Pelican to get used to fishing with this new beak. At first Pelican was embarrassed about his new look, but when he discovered its incredible use, he embraced the change.

Pelican was no longer the haughty bird he had once been. Instead of stealing all the fish from the sea, he now helped others get food they needed with his new fishing tool and generous spirit. Pelican became an even better fisherman, and although he was no longer the most handsome bird on the block, he was able to humble himself and fill the needs of his friends.

So, friend, meet challenges head-on, learn how changes can be beneficial to you, and use your talents to help others. I hope you enjoyed this story about how the pelican got his curious-looking beak and you can come back for more. Right now, you have go to school or else you'll be late!

RUNNER UP

The Things I Want to Tell You

Morgaine McEvoy

I can hear everything. Well, everything within a ten-mile radius. At least that's what my doctor said. Nobody understands exactly why. I was adopted, so they don't know if either of my biological parents have it. My doctors say it won't drastically affect me and that I should be able to live a normal life, but I'm far from normal. I notice it the most when I speak. My own voice is the loudest thing I have ever heard, and it hurts me so much. That's the reason I don't talk anymore. I never talk; I mostly write or use sign language, which I'm learning. I can't listen to music; it sounds like a tribal beating of the drums, as if something is coming and the pressure building. Sometimes, if the world gets especially loud, I have to put in earplugs and put pillows over my ears. I can still usually hear everything around me.

Since I can hear so much, and I'm so quiet, I know almost everyone's secrets. I know most of my neighbour's favourite colours, their parents' occupations and if they have ever had a gecko. Everyone finds me odd, so they ignore me and pretend I'm deaf while spilling private details to others around me. Even if they don't speak around me willingly, I hear and remember what they've said. I know the stories of so many around me, and here are only a few of them.

* * * * *

The boy that goes to the same pharmacy as I do wants to run away. He would do anything to get away from here, to be anywhere but here. He wants to be a poet, but his parents insist that he becomes a lawyer or a doctor. Something "productive" they say. They want him always to be perfect even though he can't help but fail sometimes. He wants to confide to his friends, but they can't get over the fact that he's a "typical Asian" with the same "typical" problems. He wants new friends, but he doesn't want to be the token "Asian nerd", which would be the only clique to accept him. He feels stuck.

He sometimes sneaks out of the window in his bathroom, slides down the tree in his backyard and bikes to a smoky, dark club, in downtown Guelph that hosts poetry readings every third Wednesday of the month. Last Thursday, his parents asked him about where he had gone, and since he is a terrible liar, his parents went up to his room and found his notebook, in which he wrote all his poems. His parents ripped out each page, throwing them away. It hurt him more than physical pain ever could. It felt like they were ripping out his heart. Even though he doesn't understand, his parents just want the best for him and for him to have a happy life in the hard, cruel place that they immigrated to.

I want this boy to know that he shouldn't blame his parents. Right now, it doesn't seem like his parents love him, but he's wrong. His parents do love him and just want what they think is right for him. I want this boy to know he should continue this passion and cultivate it, still with love and understanding for his parents.

* * * * *

The lady down the street from me has lived in the same house for all her life. She has never moved because instead of going to university to be a nurse, she had to stay home to help her parents when both became sick. After they both died three years ago, she inherited the large, Victorian house that has so many empty rooms that even when she's with someone, she feels alone. She lives in this house with her boyfriend, eight years older, who hurts her when she doesn't make dinner or when the chicken is too dry. Some nights, I can hear the sounds of rage as skin crashes into skin and bones. I can hear her wailing for help and the slight whimper she does when putting band-aids on her cuts. I can hear the loud screaming of her boyfriend and the slamming of the doors. She wants to leave, but she's scrounging to get by and saving for an education. She knows if she leaves her boyfriend, he will either kill himself or her.

I want this woman to know that she is strong and she is brave. I want her to know that she can do anything she sets her mind to and that I believe in her. I want her to know that there is life after being broken.

*****

The girl that has scars on her inner wrists lives four streets away from me. I can imagine her guilt and anger when she cuts herself alone in her bathroom at night. I can hear the cries of a girl who just wants to be held when she puts the bandages on her cuts and tries to fall asleep wanting to drown in her tears. I can hear her awaken early from restless nights. She told her parents who she was five months ago, and they are still refusing to listen to her. She wants them to understand that she isn't a boy. She's a girl; the daughter they've always wanted.

She wishes that she wasn't born the way she is, playing with barbies and wearing pink. She wishes her parents knew that it's not a phase and that it shatters her heart a little bit more when each day, she's referred to as "he", "him", and "Evan".

She wishes that her parents loved her for who she truly is. She wishes that she would die. She plans to kill herself next Tuesday.

I want this girl to know she is loved. I want her to know that even though we have never met, I am going to miss her and that I'm not the only one.

*****

I feel like I know these people. I want to know them, but just because I know their stories, doesn't mean I can talk to them. I want to be able to comfort them. I want to let them know that they are appreciated and loved. I want to let them know that I will always be there for them, that I will be there to tell them that voice in their head telling them that they're not worthy of anything good, is wrong. But even though I want to do these things with my whole being and heart, I never could. I could never go to them and just hold them and tell them it will be alright. I couldn't tell them why I've taken so long to be there, but I'm here now. Even if talking didn't hurt me, I would never have the confidence. Sometimes, I can't believe I'm letting innocent people die because I can't talk to them. Sometimes, I fall asleep at night crying to myself. I wonder if my hearing is a gift or a curse. I wonder if there is someone out there that can hear me crying at night. Someone, who will have more courage than I do and will come and help me. But for now, I'll sit in my room. For now, I am listening to all their stories.

RUNNER UP

Skin and Bones

Zola Senitt

Sweat trickled around the curve of my ear, a drop joining the salty puddle beginning to pool at my clavicle. Another drop fell onto my lips. I subconsciously licked it away, soothing my throat for a fraction of a second. I tried to move softly, to make up for the noise I was making with my left hand, keeping myself from flinching every time metal met metal.

"Screwdriver." My breath came in short gasps. A man in a white coat handed me a magnetic screwdriver, already with a screw stuck to its head.

I cringed, my hands still flying. After ten years of service, my hands could work as I talked. "Do you have one that's maybe not magnetic?"

"Will it interfere with your software, Kaia?" He gestured to my robotic leg, arm and eye. "No, but –"

"Then I can't supply another screwdriver. Please continue with your work." He gestured to the robot. I grumbled under my breath but listened to him. A little red light flashed in the corner of my right eye and I smiled. My alarm had gone off. The alarm told me I only had one hour left of servitude. Sixty minutes until I was free. After a year in the orphanage and ten years under "apprenticeship". I have never left my city. I knew I would get dirty looks on the streets wherever I went. I'm small for my age, and my metal limbs are not as easy to hide as some people's are. Many people will think I escaped servitude. They may even call the cyborg police on me. I'll have to keep my personal information with meat all times.

The air seal pushed open behind me. The sound echoed through the cement room. The man in the white coat walked away from me as he went to greet whoever just entered. I started to finish up the robot, the smile on my face never fading. In an hour, I would be at my new apartment, sharing stories with my other four cyborg roommates. I didn't care that no one who wasn't half metal would want to sleep anywhere close to me. I had learned a long time ago that simply letting go healed a lot of bruises. I picked up the plate that would cover the robot's wiring. I screwed in the final screws. I held up the robot proudly and turned around to see my – "Mom?"

My mother grimaced at the sound of my voice. She had probably hoped to slip in and out of the room without me noticing. "Kaia, you know you're not part of the family. Call me Mrs. Colenn."

Her haughty accent threw me for a second. I knew it was my mom. I had a photo album of our family before the accident. I smiled so brightly in those photos. I was so innocent. I thought that my family stood by me no matter what, that something like an artificial leg would made no difference. But I was wrong. One visit at the hospital was enough for my parents to give up five year old me to an orphanage, and then sign me into the cyborg slave trade at six. I was the youngest in the glass cage that the orphanage made us stand in to show us off. I was sold for two hundred dollars. I have seen thousand dollar robots treated like they were scrap metal. I am worth less than scrap metal.

"Why are you here? Did you come to –" I almost said, "say goodbye," but I caught myself. My mother – Mrs. Colenn – had made it very clear that she had no love left for me.

"The apartment you were going to move into was Prioritised." My throat tightened. There weren't enough apartments left for non-cyborgs, or "Pures", so they kicked us out. Where would I live now? "And as there are no cyborg standard housing units available, we were contacted." She grits her teeth. "Despite obvious instructions never to contact us."

The man in the white coat grimaced. "Sorry 'bout that."

"It's too late for apologies, Dr. Rose."

So that was his name. He had been my supervisor for a year now, but I hadn't bothered to learn it.

"Anyway, you are now going to come live with us."

"What?" I wasn't sure if I heard her properly.

"We live about an hour's drive from here. As you are no longer a member of our family, you will earn your keep, same as our other servants."

"Are they cyborgs, too?" I asked.

"First rule: don't ask questions. You are not part of our family. Do not act like one." Her words stung.

"Oh, okay."

"Second rule: don't talk unless you need to. You are to not be seen or heard."

I kept quiet. Talking was no doubt a violation of rule number two.

"I was told you had basic serving training at fifteen. You will proceed directly to work once you arrive. I understand you have already packed your bags?" I nodded. "Good. We will head out promptly."

So soon? I didn't even have time to say goodbye. Not that I had anyone to say goodbye to.

* * * * *

An hour later, we stood in front of what would have been my house, if it weren't for the accident. If I were still Pure. But a house barely even started to describe it. It was at least four stories tall, the windows were draped with silk curtains, the steps didn't have a speck of dust on them. I glanced down at my greasy dress. I tried to pick my prettiest dress for when I met my family, even if they're not really my family. My dress was a filthy rag no better than what they use to shine my sister's shoes. Mrs. Colenn's high heeled boots clip-clopped like a horse on the marble path leading up to the grand front door. I saw a girl in a maid's uniform peek her head from behind a curtain before scurrying away.

"Miss, you need to accompany Missus Collen to the door," The chauffeur said with a strong colony accent. I looked up in surprise. She had tilted her driver's hat precariously on her braids as soon as Mrs. Colenn turned away. Her dimples betrayed a barely concealed grin highlighted her freckles. But I didn't pay attention to the hat, the braids, or the dimples. All I could see was her robotic left eye, whose pupil rolled as it gathered information, light and colour for the brain.

"You – you're a cyborg, too?"

"Missus likes to hire us because we're cheap. Even her utter contempt for us is outweighed by the temptation to preserve her massive fortune."

"Is all the staff cyborg?"

"Not all, but most. I can show you around if you want. But first, you might want to get in. Missus does not like to be kept waiting."

I gave her a quick nod and hurried off to the door. I could see a girl standing next to a boy, both of whom looked just like me and were undoubtedly my siblings. But to them, I was a different species. I took a deep breath, and rolled up my sleeves, proudly displaying my metal arm, ready to face the family that left me behind.

RUNNER UP

Escaping My Past

Saoirse Hughes

I ran through the trees, the twigs and stones cutting my already bruised and bloody bare feet. I ran into the unknown, trying to escape from my problems. I had been thinking of running away since I was six, ever since my mother died and my father went crazy. But I was too scared. It wasn't until this morning, seven years later that I gathered up the courage to leave.

I had woken up to my father's scream as he fought with his new boss. He had already been fired from six other jobs. He was rude and always demanded more money than he worked for. I heard a door slamming. And it was suddenly quiet. He had probably scared yet another person away.

"Amaryllis! Make me breakfast!" he yelled.

I scrambled out of my blankets and put on my large grey sweater. I ran down the stairs and into the kitchen. "Good m-morning father. W-what would you like to eat?" I asked him, looking at the ground.

"Eggs and bacon." He growled.

I nodded. I started making the eggs.

"Get me some water!" he yelled.

I quickly took a cup and filled it up with cold water. I put it on the table then scrambled back to the kitchen only to be greeted with the smell of burning food. I had burned the eggs! Dad was going to be mad. And of course, he was.

"Amaryllis! What is that smell!" he shouted. I heard his heavy footsteps make their way towards me. "What did you!?" he asked menacingly.

"N-n-nothing," I lied.

"Don't lie to me, child," he said, slapping me. I winced. He always took his anger out on me.

"I b-b-burned the eggs," I said quietly.

"You useless idiot!" he yelled and slapped me so hard that I stumbled backwards.

"Scared?" he asked, staring at me as I rubbed my cheek. I shrunk back and looked at my feet. "You should be. Now make my breakfast and don't screw up this time," he said stalking off.

I hurried off and made his breakfast, careful not to mess up this time. I put his eggs and bacon on a plate and gave it to him. Then I scurried back into the kitchen and toasted a piece of toast for myself.

"Amaryllis! These eggs are tasteless!" my father yelled.

I swore to myself. I had forgotten the salt. I quickly took the container of salt and ran over to my father. I sprinkled some salt on the eggs and turned to leave.

"Ow!" I yelled as my father's hand pulled at my ponytail to turn me over to face him. He slapped me on the face. I clenched my jaw and fought back the tears.

"You can never get anything right, can you?" he said. "If you keep messing up like that, you'll be punished. And you know what my punishments are like," he said with a maniacal grin.

I didn't answer. I had been punished several times, and I never wanted that to happen again. I have cuts around my wrists from when he tied up my hands and attached me to a tree for a week, feeding me only little pieces of stale bread. My worst scars are three long white lines on my back from when he whipped me.

"Now get out of my sight!" he yelled, turning me around and pushing my head. My head whipped forward. I groaned and rubbed my neck. "What a disappointment of a child," I heard him mutter.

I raced up the stairs into my bedroom. Well, I wouldn't necessarily consider it a bedroom. It was tiny, just slightly bigger then a cupboard. My dad had sold all of my belongings, so I slept on the floor with only one blanket, and I used my clothes as a pillow. The only thing I had was a book that I kept under one of the floor boards it was my favourite book, *A Wrinkle in Time*. I also had a locket that my mother gave to me before she died. It had a picture of my mother on one side, and on the other, there was a picture of my father, before he changed.

"Amaryllis! You forgot to do the dishes!" I heard my father yell. I gasped. How could I have been so stupid? I slowly walked down the stairs, shaking. When I got to the second last stair, I saw my dad standing there, rope in hand.

"Please don't," I whispered. "I promise it will never happen again."

But he just smiled at me and started walking slowly towards the steps. I stumbled backwards and held onto the railing to stop myself from falling.

"This is what happens when you don't follow my rules," he said.

I sucked in a breath, and ran back up the stairs into my room. I locked the door and leaned against it, my heart pounding. I heard my father stomp up the stairs.

"You can't escape me," he laughed.

That's when I knew I was doomed. If he entered my room, there would be no getting out for me. I didn't have a window to climb out of, and my room was so small that he could easily corner me.

I felt the doorknob move against my back. My dad started pulling at the door knob and yelling. "You better open this up!" He wiggled at the door knob a bit more and I heard a click. He had unlocked the door. I felt him pushing against the door, and I pushed back with all my weight. But he was much stronger and pushed open the door, throwing me to the ground. He stared down at me, and I wiggled backwards, still lying on the ground.

"It's too late now," he said, then he lunged and grabbed hold of me. I squirmed and punched him, trying to escape, but it was no use. He had already tied my hands together.

"No!" I yelled.

He dragged me outside and tied me to the same tree as always.

"I'll see you in a few days," he said, and he walked back into the house.

I started crying. After my eyes dried out I realised that this time I would not be controlled and tortured by my father. This time I would escape.

I looked around at my surroundings, the forest behind my house, the never ending dead cornfields and my broken down house. I looked on the ground for anything that would be helpful. I saw a thin rusted nail.

Luckily, my hands were tied in front of me so I reached out. It was too far away. I reached out my foot and nudged the nail closer to me with my toes until it was close enough to reach out and grab. I took it in my right hand and stuck the nail underneath the rope that was around my left hand. I started rubbing it back and forth, like a saw, cutting the little fibres of the rope.

I kept sawing it, ignoring the pain on my wrists from the rope rubbing them continuously. I was now half way through the rope and the top of the nail was digging into my hand. I ignored it, determined to escape.

I gritted my teeth. Finally, the nail tore through the nail and the rope split in half. I wriggled my hands free and started undoing the knot that was around my waist, pulling until the knot slid away. Then I stood, rubbing my throbbing wrists.

I turned to look back at my house, then without taking another glance back, I dashed into the forest. I ran and ran.

That's how I got here. Running through the forest. My aching feet throbbing. Not knowing where I will go or where my path will take me. Running off to my future. Escaping my past.